GETTYSBURG:

The Story of Four Kids Whose Lives Were Changed by War

Gary L. Kaplan

Dedication

"This book is dedicated to my parents, Mickey and Vi, who raised me to believe in the good in people, and to value helping others over personal gain, and to Mrs. Rosencranz and Mrs. Rosow, early teachers who introduced me to the joys of reading and storytelling and explaining how the written word can be so informative and thought provoking.

I would be remiss if I did not also dedicate this book to the over 600,000 men and women, boys and girls, who perished during the American Civil War, and to those who lived to tell the tale afterwards, and to the many writers, essayists and teachers who bring the reality of war to us, with the message, "Why?"

Acknowledgement

"This is a book of fiction, whose characters are really a composite of many children and young adults who lived through the many battles, hardships and life changing experiences of the American Civil War. The places are real, the historical information, when based upon specific events, is true, including names of historically accurate figures, although others are purely fictional. I would like to thank the many authors who have created works of fiction and non-fiction about the American Civil War over the years, written from differing viewpoints enough to encourage this writer to dig deeper into events described herein, and into the personalities of Americans who lived to fight the fight.

There were many books that helped me along the way, giving me factual information and/or inspiration to keep going, along with numerous websites that depicted the lives of people before, during and after the war. Some of these books, include, but are not limited to, the following: The Gettysburg Nobody Knows, edited by Gabor S. Boritt; They Met At Gettysburg, by General Edward J. Stackpole; Gettysburg, by Stephen W. Sears; Catesby: Eyewitness to the Civil War, by Bob O'Connor; and The Killer Angels, by Michael Shaara. In addition, The National Archives and Library of Congress, along with the Public Broadcasting System's primary and secondary sources gave me specific information to include as I developed the characters. Not enough is written about the lives of children who endured the hardships of war, losing loved ones, their homes, and even their lives. This book is in part paying homage to their memories.

Gratitude also goes to the many teachers, parents, and students, past and present with whom I interacted during the writing of this novel. I respect their opinions about the content and writing style, both negative and positive, and their insights, and without their interest and input I could not have finished. They also helped me to understand the pressures of writing a novel, finding time to think, create, write, rewrite, and cast aside my own self-doubts that accompanied me as a first- time writer.

And, I would be remiss in not giving thanks to my family. To my sister, Sharon, for her belief in my ability to write, and to my brother in law, Andy, whose own writing inspired me to put my own pen to paper. To my children, Allye and Zack, who believe in expressing themselves with confidence and authority and urged me to continue; and to my wife, Beth, who encouraged me along the way and who put up with my frequent trips to our local library resale shop, my second home, and whose comments: "enough Civil War books already," provided enough mirth to ease the pressures of those late nights of pondering what to write next and which kept me grounded. Thank you all, although thanks are never enough.

Gary L. Kaplan, 2017.

Section One

Sarah

"**M**omma, Momma, I'm cold," whispered Sarah as she lay close to her mother, covered only with a threadbare, woolen blanket. The slight breeze through the open window had chilled during the night causing the air in the bedroom to become much cooler than when they first took to the bed. "Hush, child," her mother said. "You know that since your daddy left, we have to maintain this place as best we can, and right now we are out of firewood. Just get closer to me and give me a hug; that will warm you up." Sarah did so as she moved closer to her mother, pulling the blanket up over her shoulders, hoping to get some more precious minutes of sleep before the day's chores started.

Ever since John Woodbury left to join the Confederate army, the Woodbury farm had fallen in disarray, what with the white farmhands joining John, and the black servants either too ill or not directed enough to do their work. Without John or their overseer, Mr. Streeter, who had also left to join the Confederacy despite his advanced age and slight limp in his walk, to force the workers to complete their daily tasks, their productivity declined and the farm ceased to produce saleable crops. Firewood was at a premium too, since the Confederate army had been confiscating as much as they could for the war effort. Equally important to the military were spare machinery parts, stored foodstuffs, and even horses and mules. In fact, many small farms were being victimized in this same way with the Army coming around in numbers to collect whatever could be taken from the farms, regardless of the need of the farmers.

"I hate this war, Tilly," said Sarah, in her best grown up voice. "It has brought us nothing but grief, and I miss Poppa, too." (Tilly, that was what her mother, friends, and husband, John called her, and was sometimes used by Sarah when she was trying to act a bit older.) Tilly's real name was Mathilda, but she stopped using that formal name years ago. She preferred Tilly, the name her father began calling her when she was ten years old, and it had stuck ever since despite the protests of her mother. She was a stern yet compassionate woman of fine breeding who believed in strict formality around the house.

Yes, she preferred Tilly, except when she went into town for provisions; then she was called Ms. Woodbury by the local folk. She missed her Poppa too, and she missed the way of life on the farm before John left, before the War began. They would sit on the steps leading up to the porch of the house, sipping cold lemonade on those hot, lazy South Carolina afternoons and Sarah would be playing on the grass with her dolls and her dog, Simply. He was named Simply because, well, he was simply the cutest little beagle she had ever seen and she kind of adopted that name.

"Child," Tilly offered, "we have to get up soon and tend to the chickens. There should be enough eggs out in the hen house now for breakfast, and we don't want to have them all of a sudden disappear. The servants are hungry too and they need to get their share of the eggs as well.

Tilly did not like to call the servants "slaves"; raised in the North, where slavery was not sanctioned, she was told that people were people, some good, some bad, but all equal, even the dark-skinned ones they saw down at the lumber yard where her father worked as a foreman. She especially liked one; they called him Big Mike. She had known him for a long time, long before she met John. He was tall, strong as an ox, and one of the free, black men who worked in the yard. He was really as gentle as a butterfly. As long as you didn't cross him! Tilly began to recall to herself a particular story from her childhood. She did so from time to time to take her mind off the events of the day, with her frustration growing being alone on the farm without a husband and best friend.

Her father had told her about the time when three strangers showed up at the lumberyard looking for Mr. St. Clair, the owner. They said that Mr. St. Clair had promised them some jobs and they were there to follow up on his promise. These men were all dressed like they hadn't changed their clothes for a week; all dusty and greasy looking, unshaven, and each was more sinister looking than the other. Her father told them that Mr. St. Clair had gone out of town, on some kind of business trip he said. Well, they didn't believe her daddy, so he said, so they began pushing him around and knocking some books, papers and other supplies off the counter.

Apparently, they were making enough noise that Big Mike, heard them and he came a runnin' into the office, his hat flying off of his head as he entered the room. "What do YOU want, darkie," said one of the men, the one who seemed to be the leader. "Why nothin' sir", said Big Mike, as he eyed daddy and then eyed the men. He knew something was wrong. "OK, then you can leave," said the first man who spoke. "This ain't none of your business." Yea," said another man, slightly smaller and younger than the first, but equally as sinister looking. He was holding a knife, kind of like a bowie knife but not as long, in his hand. "This ain't none of your business, and if you don't leave right away and mind your business, you can taste the tip of this here knife." And then the man held up his hand as if to throw the knife.

Daddy said that Big Mike moved so fast, he created a blur. At six feet and four inches, and hands as big as meat cleavers, Big Mike must have been a sight to see. He jumped forward, knocked the knife out of the man's hand with his left hand, grabbed the man by the neck with his right hand, lifted him off the ground and pushed him back into the third man. The veins in Big Mike's neck were now bulging as if they were ready to burst and his eyes were aflame like burning bushes. The men were not expecting this type of reaction and looked mighty scared. They looked at each other, let my daddy go and ran out of the office, never to be seen again. From that day on, daddy referred to Big Mike as his friend, and told us that no matter what his skin color was, he was to be trusted and treated with respect.

As Tilly recalled this story, she thought about how she first met John Woodbury, a fine, mild mannered, handsome man who had come to the lumberyard looking for some provisions for his farm in South Carolina. He had been referred to Mr. St. Clair by a friend, and had made the trip up North both to purchase goods and to see that part of the country. You see, he had never been North of the Carolinas before and was curious about life up North.

John had been born and raised in Kings County, South Carolina, and had lived there his whole life, growing up and working the farm owned by his father. John was an only child and as such, worked all the various chores on the farm, from collecting eggs from the chicken coop, bailing hay, feeding the animals, even helping cook when his mother was too tired or too sick. She died when John was a teenager, and John had to assume a larger role on the farm. John had seen many larger farms and plantations in South Carolina and often thought about how his life might have been different, perhaps a bit easier, if they had more land, more workers and more money.

When his father passed away, John, rather than selling the farm, took it over and began building it up, acquiring some neighboring land from Mr. Thorogood, a kindly but old man who could no longer work his own land. John paid Mr. Thorogood a good price for the land, and also acquired the slaves that were owned by Mr. Thorogood. John was not mean-spirited, nor was he a firm believer in slavery; he was simply a farmer who did what he had to do and having slaves was just the way of life back then. He disliked calling them slaves. Actually, he had grown up with several who had been born on the farm, and John considered them more like friends than slaves. Still, according to custom, he was the boss and they were still owned by him and as he took over the farm and its production, he came to see them less as friends and more like a necessary commodity.

"Momma, I'm getting hungry, can we go get them eggs?" Tilly didn't respond; her mind was somewhere a long time ago. "Momma, didn't you hear me?" repeated Sarah, as she tugged on Tilly's sleeve. Tilly gathered herself, feeling guilty about ignoring Sarah as she was thinking about the past. "Sure honey, get your overalls on, wash your face and meet me at the barn." Sarah jumped out of the cold bed (since John left, she had let Sarah share her bed both for warmth and for Sarah's peace of mind), and went to the other room where the pitcher, bowl, and water were kept. With her long, auburn colored hair flowing behind her, Sarah ran to the pitcher of water and poured some in the porcelain bowl, the one that her mother had gotten from her father as a gift. It was white porcelain with blue colored pictures of little fairies dancing in rows around the bowl. Sarah liked to think of herself dancing like one of those fairies, all care free and having fun. She dipped her hands in the water, still cool from the night, and splashed her face before she grabbed a towel from the rack to wipe off. She didn't like to use soap as she had heard that too much soap would dry her skin, but she didn't tell her mother.

Tilly got up from the bed, pulled back the sheets and the blanket, straightening them just like her mother had taught her to do, trying to make the bed more presentable. She wasn't expecting any guests, but she was intent on keeping things around the house as neat as she could. She then straightened herself, and looked in the mirror and saw a face that once had been young and beautiful. Her naturally shiny, black hair had become dull-looking. Now, with the worry of the war, the sorrowful conditions of the farm and the fears that accompanied her daily work schedule, her face had become drawn, pale, and filled with small wrinkles around her eyes and mouth. She looked too at Sarah, who was just growing into herself and was no longer a little toddler, but a young teen, with that long, rich, auburn colored hair; the same color hair her father had and with skin like fine, polished alabaster. She wished she could comfort Sarah more, and tell her that all would be well, and HER daddy would be home soon. She couldn't though; she didn't know where he was and she wasn't sure what was going to happen, but she kept up the appearance of being calm and self- assured so as not to upset Sarah.

Oh, how she hated the war too. It did more than change her lifestyle, and her relationships with her neighbors and friends; it destroyed the dreams she had built for their family and for their future. Yes, she hated the war too hoping daily that it would come to an end and she would see John walking up the road to the farmhouse.

Section Two

Joshua

Joshua couldn't believe how hot it was, even at 9:00 in the morning. He had been up since sunup, as he was every day during the week and most Saturdays, as he labored on the Andrews plantation. You see, Joshua was a slave boy, merely a teenager, but like all the other slaves, young and old, he had to work in the fields all day, sun or no sun, getting in the cotton so it could be cleaned, processed and brought to market. Mr. Andrews (Peter was his given name, although the workers on the plantation, when allowed to, would call him Massah) was the owner of this very large, and very well-organized cotton plantation. Plantations of this size need help of course, and in South Carolina, slaves were the work force. Joshua was large for his age, standing nearly six feet tall, but still thin as a rail. Wearing a tattered shirt, a hand- me- down from some older slave, with a torn collar and grease stained sleeves, and britches made from wool scraps pieced together with yarn, he would lumber around the plantation doing whatever his job was for the day, always on the lookout for an extra piece of clothing or some discarded pair of shoes. His were filled with holes and were a mite tight on his ever-growing feet.

South Carolina has long been a cotton rich state, from its beginnings after the American Revolution, when its farmers and businessmen realized how much cotton was in demand overseas. The British and French merchants were willing to pay almost any price for finely grown and cleaned cotton. Ever since Mr. Whitney (that's Eli Whitney, the inventor of the cotton gin in 1793) provided cotton growers with a machine to multiply the amount of cotton that could be cleaned after being picked from the fields almost five-fold, cotton production became so large of an industry in the South that the phrase, "Cotton is King," was coined. Of course, with the ability to clean more cotton at a much faster pace, growers needed more help to pick the cotton from the fields.

Now, pickin' cotton is no easy task; it takes hours of walking the fields, picking the soft, white puffy clouds from their prickly plants. Mr. Andrews was one of the most proficient providers of cotton to the mills in the whole state of South Carolina. Like his daddy before him, and his daddy before that, Mr. Andrews followed in a long line of plantation owners who were responsible for the vast cotton trade. From that trade, his family became very wealthy.

He was able to accomplish this for he had almost one hundred workers who would go out daily in the fields, with canvas bags, and stoop and pick that cotton from sunrise to sunset, with a little break in the middle for some rest and nourishment. These laborers were called slaves, although Mr. Andrews referred to them as his "boys" or "girls."

Joshua knew this story all too well, as he had been born on the Andrews plantation over fourteen years ago and began working in the fields at the age of nine. Before that, he did his chores in the Andrews house, fetching eggs from the chicken coop, sweeping the floors, emptying trash; really any chore that Mrs. Andrews had him do. His momma would sit with him at night and tell him how she first came to live on the plantation years ago, before Joshua was born, and how his daddy had been there too. His daddy was one of Mr. Andrews' strongest and most reliable "pickers" and he took much pride in bringing in more than his fair share of cotton each day. Mr. Andrews seemed to like Jake. Mr. Andrews never did ask him his real name after he first acquired Poppa from a neighbor, Mr. Weatherford.

Some time ago, so Joshua was told, Mr. Weatherford owed Mr. Andrews some money for some seed that Mr. Andrews had left over from a planting. Mr. Weatherford couldn't afford to pay Mr. Andrews back when the debt became due. His farm was not prospering, what with his wife ill, his two sons off to the War and the lack of good irrigation on his land which caused his crops to wither and die. So, after surveying the land, and thinking about Mr. Weatherford and his problems, Mr. Andrews said: "Thomas, I'll tell you what I can do. I do need the money, that is for sure. But, I also need some more help in my fields. I will agree to forgive the debt you owe me if you go ahead and give me that slave over there, and his woman. You know which slave I mean; the one with the big, broad shoulders, the darkie who lives with that woman who does your cooking."

Now, Mr. Weatherford didn't want to part with John, nor his woman, Mattie, but knowing how conditions were, he really had no choice. He could have his daughter, Molly, take over the cooking and cleaning in the house, so his wife, Esther could rest. The doctors said she shouldn't spend time in the sun, or do any heavy work as her health was not good. Molly was only seventeen, but had spent much time helping out in the kitchen and around the house since her mother took ill and was more than able to assume the role of matron of the house.

Mr. Weatherford agreed to the deal; the two men had a paper drawn up and they each signed it and gave a copy to Mr. Alexander Buford, the local lawyer in town just in case there was a problem with the agreement down the road. Mr. Buford agreed, explained to the two men all the particulars of the agreement and congratulated them on their good negotiations. After all, an agreement duly negotiated and sealed is much better than a disagreement later between neighbors. The men wanted to stay friendly, and it seemed that they both benefited by the deal. So, Mr. Buford had his secretary bring in some refreshments. She poured three glasses of whiskey and then the men toasted to each other on the completion of their arrangement.

When John, or Jake, as Mr. Andrews now called Poppa, (for Mr. Andrews was not real keen on using names that someone else had given to a slave,) came over to the Andrews property, he brought momma and some provisions; just some old clothing, a little dried pork and rice and an old pile of canvas bags to help with the picking. Mr. Weatherford would not need them anymore.

What neither man knew at the time, and what bothered Mr. Weatherford when he found out, was that momma had me a brewin' in her tummy. Even Momma and Poppa did not know, but after a few months living with Mr. Andrews, Momma started getting sick and a mite weak. She couldn't work in the field any longer so Mr. Andrews had Jake go into town with the overseer, Mr. Potts, to fetch the doctor, the same one who also treated Mrs. Weatherford. Well, after the doctor examined Momma, which was really a rare occurrence as most often, slaves didn't have the advantage of being looked after by a real doctor, the doctor said to Mr. Andrews, "Peter (that was Mr. Andrews' given name), it looks like you are going to have another field hand working for you!"

"What do you mean by that, Dr. Smith?" "Well, Peter, this here young lady is soon to give birth, and if my prediction holds true, it will be a boy." "And, by the looks of the daddy and momma, he will be healthy and strong. Now, you just see to it that this woman takes care of herself, or she will lose that baby, and you will lose a valuable investment."

Momma would remind me of that story time and again, as she wanted me to know the history of where I came from, just as she remembered where she came from, and her momma and poppa too! She also wanted me to remember what happened to Poppa and why he wasn't on the plantation anymore, and why she never did trust Mr. Andrews. But she became flustered and didn't finish her story this time.

"Son, you had better get yourself cleaned up and ready for dinner. You know how Mr. Andrews wants everything ready on the table for dinner."

I guess I had been daydreaming a bit, for I had forgotten that today was Saturday and Massah (oh, how I hated calling Mr. Andrews that name) always had his nearest neighbors join him for dinner on Saturdays and all us "boys" had to help with the food gettin' and the servin' of the meal. "Joshua, your special clothes are in the back room, behind the kitchen as usual. Now you hurry and take care of business."

"All right momma, "I said. And as I ran through the kitchen, I could smell the chicken cookin' in the oven, and thought to myself what it would be like to be to be able to sit down at the table and eat with a fork and knife and plate and take all the time I wanted. I wouldn't have to hear Mr. Potts yelling, yet again, "Joshua, get your hind end out of that kitchen and get back to the wagon. You have some more work to do. Those sacks of cotton have to go into the barn and you are the fastest worker I have."

Before he left the kitchen, Joshua hesitated a bit. He looked out the window at those wide fields and those wooden fences with that sharp wire across the top, and he also saw old Mr. Potts with his sweaty, baggy clothes and whip, droopy moustache, and greasy, long brown hair that fell over his eyes. He had the smell of the fields and the animals and it was a smell Joshua never could get used to. Some day, some day, he thought. Some day I will see what is out there, beyond those fences, even if it takes the rest of my days.

Section Three

Martin

"C'mon father," said Martin. "Can't we do this tomorrow?"
"No, son," said Martin's father, Samuel Wickham, a prominent citizen of Westfield, New York, and the town's long-time mayor. "Time is wasting, and we have much to do." Mr. Wickham was also the owner of Wickham's Foundry, for many years, the area's leading producer of iron works for construction of farm equipment, and more recently, since the beginning of the war, the local manufacturer of rifles and cannon for the Federals.

The site for the foundry was ideal. The nearby, rapidly flowing Somerset River provided enough water to power the foundry. There was plenty of timber for fuel available from the acres of forest near the town and iron ore from local quarries was easily gotten and provided many jobs for the local residents, those who had not gone off to war. Given that transporting arms and munitions was difficult, the river's proximity to the foundry proved to be a reliable route for the boats to travel as they delivered their loads southward.

Mr. Wickham had been hired, no actually Wickham's Foundry had been hired, by the government to supply the Army of the Potomac (which was the name given to the Union, or Northern forces since the beginning of the War between the States) with munitions for the support of the troops. Instrumental in the production of cannon for the war effort, the foundry manufactured several types of artillery pieces, including the Rodman and Dahlgren cannons and most importantly, the Parrott gun, named after Robert P. Parrott, a former Army captain. These guns became the most often used artillery pieces of the war and Wickham's Foundry was now the prime supplier.

Mr. Wickham had been a long-time supporter of Mr. Lincoln's policy of saving the Union, and believed that the best way to do so would be to let the states who seceded from the Union know that the North would not run out of munitions. Mr. Wickham, without letting his son, Martin, know, had not only pledged his company's assets, but also his personal wealth, to the support of the Northern forces. Ever since his mother had died nearly three years ago, Martin had seen his father become more and more involved in his work, paying little attention to Martin's needs or wants.

Growing up in upstate New York, Martin had little connection with what was going on in the War, in the South, or in the secret meetings that Martin's father would have in their home almost weekly. He recognized some of the people who would come, many of Mr. Wickham's friends and businessmen from town, but not all. He especially took notice of the free black men who would come, seemingly nervous about being there but always polite and soft-spoken, as if there were some secretive going on.

"But father, I wanted to go down to Blake's Landing to do some late afternoon fishing; you know how those fish bite as the sun gets low in the sky and the mosquitoes and dragonflies start to hover over the water." "Martin," Mr. Wickham responded, "We have so much more to do. Fishing can wait. Our supply order is behind and we have to get the next shipment out by tomorrow."

"Yes sir," Martin said, knowing that he really had no choice. He was his father's chief packer, and even at the age of 16, young for foundry workers, he was the best. He grew up in the business, watching his father's every move for the past five years. Martin was the spitting image of his father. His long brown hair tucked into his cap matched the color of his eyes, and he was big for his age, bigger than most of his friends in town. He also had the dark complexion that he inherited from his mother, who had some Indian blood in her. Oh, how he longed to be able to hear once again her stories about her childhood. She was raised in the Western territories before she came to New York as a young girl to escape from the harshness of life in the West.

Martin knew that he could work faster than any of the other employees at the foundry, and he was proud of that. He had even won a contest once with Sam Forest, one of Wickham's oldest employees, and a long- time packer, to see who could pack and seal the most rifles into the wooden boxes, complete with straw and spare parts, to be delivered to New York for shipment South to the forces that were stationed around Washington.

Martin knew the importance of his work, but also hoped that this war would end soon, as his father said it might. Since the war started, his father had paid little attention to him. He also wondered why his father kept having these weekly meetings. He was not used to having strangers in his home, but by now it seemed that it had become a regular occurrence and yet, still a mystery to him.

He had heard of other houses in town where people would gather to discuss the War at night. Some of the most respected men in town would be there, all with important looking satchels that contained, well, he didn't know what they contained. All he knew was that he was getting real tired of working in the foundry when boys his age were leaving the area, trying to find work in other areas. Or, so their parents were told.

Martin had a friend, Billy Bonham, who had left just last month. Martin had heard from some of his school buddies that Billy really didn't go to look for a job. He was headed South to enlist in the First New York militia, bound to fight those rebs who were trying to tear the country apart with their pleas for states' rights. Martin knew though that the real reason those southern states seceded was because of slavery. They simply wanted to keep their way of life going, and Mr. Lincoln said no, enough of that.

"I wonder what it would be like to carry one of these rifles over my shoulder and join the fight," Martin thought to himself. He didn't dare mention this to his father, for he knew what his father would say: "Martin, you are too far removed from that War to even think about this. We have a business to run, and I will have no part in sending you off. Besides, you are way too young to take part in this foolish endeavor (meaning the War between the States.) Let the War be fought by those older and wiser than you." "I don't know why those southerners keep on with their fighting. Don't they know that they are outgunned, outmanned, and don't have the funds to keep fighting?"

Still, Martin would sometimes lay in his bed at night, look out at the stars through his window, and imagine himself, along with some other soldiers, running across a field, dodging bullets, or bayonets, and escaping from the drudgery of the factory. He also wondered about those secret meetings. What could be going on? What were they talking about? Whenever he asked his father, Mr. Wickham would simply say: "Martin, those meetings are none of your concern. You best mind your own business and let us men mind ours." If only he could listen one night to what they were saying. If only he could get close enough to listen to their words. If only... but then his eyes would close, the wondering stopped and sleep would overcome him.

Section Four

Abigail

Abigail had never seen this much rain before. The streets of Washington had become rivers of mud, leaves, tree branches and all kinds of debris washed away from the front yards of homes owned by even the most prominent members of Washington society. No one was immune from the storms, and Abigail felt especially sorry for the rows and rows of soldiers lined up on both sides of the street, as she looked down Pennsylvania Avenue. With little but their canvas tent covers to shield them from the rain and wind, if they even had any, for some did not, they slowly made their way down Pennsylvania Avenue, hoping to get a glance of Mr. Lincoln before they moved out of town towards, gosh, who knew where.

There were also double lines of army wagons, some carrying provisions for the soldiers, some carrying wounded men headed for the hospitals. Regardless of their cargo, or their mission, they navigated around and through the mud and debris on the street. She also saw a number of young black boys, carrying little boxes of bootblack, brushes and the like, ready to assist in wiping down the boots of visitors to the White House, just down the road past the Willard Hotel and near the Department of the Treasury.

She was hoping to meet Mr. Lincoln one day; perhaps her father or mother would take her one Saturday, as Saturdays were public reception days at the White House. She had never been inside, and thought about how she would enjoy such a visit, and maybe even meet Mrs. Lincoln too, all fashionably dressed and made up as she greeted guests to her "home." Mrs. Lincoln enjoyed having visitors come to the White House. It gave her relief from watching her husband so concerned about the War and all its happenings.

Abigail knew full well that the War was going on; she had been listening to her father and mother talk about the War almost daily. Ever since they moved to Washington when Abigail was eight years old, her family had been involved in government work. Her father, John Handy, had been brought from Pittsburgh to assist in President Buchanan's administration. Mr. Handy had been a successful administrator in Pittsburgh's largest commercial real estate firm, and was very active in local politics.

After Mr. Lincoln won the election in 1860, and took office in 1861, his advisors had told him about Mr. Handy, and how skilled he was at keeping records, dispatching employees when needed to different work sites, and how his organizational skills could aid Mr. Lincoln. Most recently, Mr. Handy had been appointed an Assistant Secretary in the newly established Department of Agriculture, and his importance was not lost on his daughter. Still, Abigail missed the times when she and her father and mother would take off on Sunday afternoons for picnics in the many parks in and around Pittsburgh, and she also thought about and missed her friends from her school. They would go and play dress up, imagining themselves to be fine ladies, serving tea to each other and discussing the happenings of the day. Life certainly was different now for a fourteen- year old girl in Washington, D.C. with the uncertainties of war looming all around.

"Abigail, could you please stop staring at those poor boys down the street and come here and help me with the cleaning?" Abigail's mother spoke up. "This work is not getting any easier, and I could certainly use your help."

Mrs. Molly Handy, Abigail's mother, was well aware of Abigail's sensitivities. She knew that Abigail was a kind and considerate young girl. Abigail actually had a habit for caring for stray animals whenever she could, finding food for them and sometimes even finding a friend to take care of them if she could not. How many times they would have visitors to their home and Abigail would burst into the drawing room and say to their guests, "Could you please help us with this little dog?" She would then produce a scraggly, long-haired dog that was more often than not underfed, or ailing from some unknown malady. She would then just look at the guest with those shining blue eyes, matched against her silken blond hair, hold the dog in her arms, and, well, who could deny her request!

Before you knew it, the guest was leaving with yet another one of Abigail's orphans. Now that the storms had become increasingly strong, more and more such orphans were showing up at the Handy residence. As long as Abigail could hide them down in the cellar, away from Mr. Handy, she could do her best to take care of them and to find them homes.

"Mother," Abigail said soon after the latest rainstorm had passed, "would it be alright if I go to visit Rachel?" Mrs. Handy knew that Rachel was Abigail's best friend and had become so ever since they moved to Washington. She lived just a couple of streets over from their house, and Rachel's father worked in the same building with Mr. Handy. Since the storms began, and with the war going on, however, Abigail didn't really get out much, so she thought it might be a good idea to allow Abigail to go.

"Abby, you can go but be sure to take this umbrella with you. You don't know when the rain may start again. And, be sure to wear those boots in the corner by the window. That mud is pretty nasty. And, stay clear of those soldiers! You never know…" "Mother, could you please stop treating me like a child?" "I know the best way to get to Rachel's house and avoid those soldiers. Besides, now that the rain has stopped, Rachel and I can look for more of those strays. At least HER father is more reasonable in letting Rachel help out taking care of those cats and dogs!"

"Now, Abigail, that is not fair. You know how hard your father works and how he needs his peace and quiet at night. When he arrives home, the last thing he wants to hear or see is a bunch of mangy critters brought in by his very well-meaning, but not very practical daughter." Mrs. Handy could hardly keep the smile from erupting on her face as she said this, and she thought of how lucky she was to have such a considerate daughter and how happy Abigail seemed to be when she devoted herself to this animal recovery service of hers. Yes," Mrs. Handy said to herself, "she is so much like me!"

Since the War began, and all the restrictions were imposed on them, Abigail's life was not nearly the same as it had been in Pittsburgh and the little pleasures that she experienced could be tolerated. Even so, Mrs. Handy asked Robert, their houseman, to secretly look over Abigail as she ventured out. She often spoke to the other mothers in town about the hardships they were experiencing, especially the ones with daughters, and how careful they have to be with their safety.

"Robert, don't let Abigail know you are looking after her. Just keep an eye out and if you see anything that disturbs you, just step up and let her know you are there. Here, take this bag with you. You can say that you were just going to do some shopping for the house, and my, what a coincidence that you ran into her!"

Mrs. Handy continued, "She might not believe you, but knowing Abigail, she would be just as happy knowing you were there than not, although she probably would not admit it. You know how much she adores you and your stories. Ever since she was little and you came to work for us in Pittsburgh, Abigail has taken to you. And when you came with us to Washington, well, she was just thrilled that you could join us.

You have become an important part of her life, and I can see how you share the same feelings about her when you talk to her about your life on that plantation in South Carolina and how you escaped and made your way up North. Thank goodness for those good people on the Underground Railroad who gave you assistance. It certainly is too bad that your wife could not leave with you. But such a perilous journey most likely would have been much too difficult for her. We want you to know how much we appreciate your being with us, as a free man, and promise that we will do all we can to help you find your family. Mr. Handy has Mr. Lincoln's ear, and we are all against that cursed slavery."

Robert listened, knowing that Mrs. Handy was being kind and truthful and he really did feel like part of the family, or as much as a former slave could feel in a house of white people, no matter how friendly and warm they could be.

He still had memories of plantation life as a young man. From time to time he would wake in the middle of the night, his eyes wide open, sweat dripping off his face, and his body shaking as those horrible memories came back. The memories of screams, of beatings, of sights so terrible that he could not even tell Mr. or Mrs. Handy, let alone Abigail. What good would it do now? They must be part of the past. But still, he could not give up hope that some day, he would see his wife again. Some day.

Section Five

The War

America had long been known as the land of opportunity. Opportunity for all, or, maybe not quite all. Ever since the writing of the Declaration of Independence, drawn up by Mr. Thomas Jefferson long ago, not every person who lived and breathed the air of this fine country had the benefit of freedom. Because of the pressures put upon the Constitutional Convention delegates from South Carolina and its sister colonies, "all men are created equal" was a term that was meant to apply to only white men. Over the years since, and especially in the deep South, the term "equal" meant different things to different people: it did not apply to those dark-skinned people; men, women, and children, originally brought to the shores of America by Dutch traders in 1619 to work the farms and fields, nor to their successors.

Generations of these enslaved people were bought and sold to plantation owners across the South to work the fields, free from wages or of any rights for self-preservation, except for what they could hide away, far from the view of their "masters." Whole families had been sold, or torn apart, without regard to individual feelings or the needs of those families.

Ever since the infamous Dred Scott case (Dred Scott v. Sandford) was heard by the U.S. Supreme Court and the decision issued by Chief Justice Taney in 1857, the black man was to be considered property, to be dealt with like a piece of furniture or a farm mule; he had no right to sue, to speak up against a master, to marry, to raise his own children or to work his own property. Unlike what was happening in the North where freedom for the blacks was more tolerable, the southern black, and the way of life in the South, was like being in another world.

In fact, this division between the North and South became so strong, so widely practiced and so powerful, that beginning in late 1860, led by South Carolina, several southern states actually separated themselves from the Union. They seceded, or withdrew from the Union, and formed their own government, and called themselves the Confederate States of America. Led by Jefferson Davis, a former graduate of West Point, the nation's premier military academy, these states felt that their way of life, their very existence, depended upon the continuation of slavery, their "peculiar institution", and they did not want any interference from the North.

As their economy was essentially agrarian, different from the industrial nature of the North, the people in the South needed to continue operating their farms and plantations with the use of slaves. No longer able to conduct a slave trade (not since 1808, when it was made illegal) these southern states did not want their northern counterparts to interfere with their "peculiar institution" of slavery. Ever since the shelling of Fort Sumter, in

April of 1861, the South began to build up an army in support of its cause. Despite the protestations of Mr. Lincoln, elected as President of the Union in 1860 with barely a 40% share of the popular vote, the South continued to demand its independence from the Union as a whole, and vowed to keep its way of life, slavery and all.

Unfortunately, people and families were divided upon the issue of slavery, of states' rights and upon the entry into war. Brother was often pitted against brother, parent against child, cousin against cousin, neighbor against neighbor. There was no right, there was no wrong; there was just the war and all its misguided glory and its misery.

At first, it was thought that the war, or the skirmish, as it was originally called, would be short. But after the debacle at the First Battle of Bull Run (or First Manassas as it was called in the South) where the troops of the North were forced to flee the battlefield, past well-dressed men and women who had left Washington for the day, out to see the "festivities" of the war in their wagons or on horseback, the North was awakened to the significance of the efforts put forth by the Southern war machine. The North also realized that this so-called skirmish would probably be not too short after all.

The Northern troops also became familiar with the infamous "Rebel yell," a new and previously unknown blood curdling war cry used by the southern troops as they rushed over fields and farmland toward their new enemy. Sometimes ill equipped with armaments, this Rebel yell often proved the difference between success and failure on the fields of battle, as the sound and fury of the yell made grown men cringe and fall back in retreat.

Men (and some women by most accounts) joined the forces in the North and the South; some for glory, some to protect the home front, some to preserve the Union, some to preserve a way of life, some merely for adventure. Quickly he ranks ballooned in numbers, adding people like Mr. John Woodbury of South Carolina who joined the infantry, along with neighbors and friends, despite the protestations of his wife and daughter. "This is something I have to do," said Mr. Woodbury, as he enlisted and said goodbye to Tilly and Sarah at the train station near their farm.

It has been nearly two years now since word had first come back from Mr. Woodbury. Was he alive? Was he dead? After two long and bloody years, 1863 was now a year filled with anxiety, despair and bewilderment for all, both North and South. No one knew what would lie ahead, and certainly not for a group of four young people living in very different circumstances.

Section Six

Sarah's Plan

While standing on the front porch of their aging house, with the withering plants needing care, the floor boards drying out and cracked, filled with slivers just waiting to jab someone in the foot, and the vistas of the fields, slowly drying up and devoid of help, Tilly and Sarah talked about their future. "Sarah," cautioned Tilly, "I am not sure how much longer we can stay here on this farm. The crops are just about lost and we can't afford to keep throwing seed down in the dirt with no one to till the soil or care for the plants that are still here. Why, just yesterday, I heard that the last of our workers was leaving, going to look for somewhere else to live and work and I could not stop them," she added.

"But Momma, I am sure that Daddy will come back soon," Sarah responded, as she, too, wondered how they were going to make ends meet. Just last week, Sarah noticed that they had received a letter from the bank addressed to her parents. She discreetly opened the envelope and read that they were far behind in their payments for the money they borrowed last year, when things were beginning to fail. They would have to make some payments soon, or the bank threatened to have them evicted. "Momma, what does it mean to be evicted?" questioned Sarah. Even though she was receiving a good education from her mother, her sometime tutor, Ms. Ingram, who lived down the road and often would stop by to see Sarah and spend time with her, and the many newspapers she was able to get from the postman, she was not keen on many of the words that "professionals" used.

"Sarah, eviction means that because we can't afford to make our full payments to the bank, they might have to make us leave the farm and take it over. They would probably then sell it off to someone with money to cover our debt. If your daddy were here, I am sure he would stop it, but he isn't. I have written to my father and mother for help, but I haven't heard anything back from them yet. I am sure they have their own problems, with the war and everything, and they most likely could not help anyway."

"I think it is time we really consider making some changes," offered Tilly, as she gave Sarah a great big hug and drew her close to her. Tilly could not help but see the tears that were beginning to well up in Sarah's eyes.

Tilly did not want to leave the farm; it had been in the Woodbury family for ages. What if John did come home soon? But what if the war continued and the Yankees (the term given to the soldiers from the North) came all the way down here. Then what? Still, she didn't want to worry Sarah any more than she already had.

"Sarah, I am going to write to my cousin, Sally Mayberry. She lives up north in Pennsylvania, and maybe she can offer some help. I know she has a lot of land and although we haven't spoken or written to each other in several years, we were real close once. She comes from a big family and I reckon she might be able to help us, or at least offer some advice.

"You mean, she can give us some money?" Sarah responded, excitedly. "No, I don't want to ask her for money Sarah." "Maybe we can go visit her on the farm for a while. I hear that Pennsylvania has some really nice land, it's not so hot up there, and Sally also has a daughter just about your age. They don't have a plantation, but I remember that they were raising horses at one time. They even had some ponies for the kids to ride. I will send her a letter tomorrow, Sarah, and see how she responds. I think we need to get away from here for a while anyway. I can tell our neighbor that if Daddy comes back while we are gone, he can come and join us. I will let Mrs. Ingram know as well, as she really enjoys working with you and I am sure she will miss you."

By the look on Sarah's face, one of gradual acceptance, Tilly thought that Sarah sounded agreeable to her plan. She wondered though: How were they going to travel from South Carolina to Pennsylvania? How would they get past the Yankees without being caught? What if they were captured? How long would it take to get there? What if Sally didn't want them there? Tilly was beginning to get a headache from all her wondering and decided to stop thinking about it for now. Maybe the bank would not evict them. Maybe she could hold them off a little longer. Still, she decided that she would write Sally anyway. There were too many maybes for her now to consider.

Sarah returned to her room and wondered too! Did she want to leave the farm? What would happen to all her things here? She had heard that some people in the valley had left their farms, plantations and houses because of the war; she wasn't sure if she was really agreeable to the plan to go to Pennsylvania. What was Pennsylvania like? How would they get there? What about Daddy?

She looked around her room and remembered the time that they put curtains on her window, those nice, lacy, blue curtains that they had gotten downtown. Her father had no real concern for the color, but Sarah and Tilly decided that the blue would fit in well with her white and blue bedding. From her bedroom window, the blue curtains would also pick up the color of the blue sky in the afternoon as the sun cast its glow on the house and the adjoining fields. Sarah liked having her own room, where she used to go and play pretend with her dolls and put on her little tea parties. Now, things were different, and her room was a place to go to get away from the worries of the time.

She began to cry and fell upon her bed. "Oh, I wish all this fighting would just stop and that Daddy would come home and we could be like it was before he left," she sobbed. "I want to stay here, stay in my home and be near my friends." She began to speak out loud. She didn't care if anyone heard her. She knew how she felt. Maybe there was some other way, she thought. Maybe I could go into town and talk to the people at the bank. Surely, they would listen to me, or so she thought. "I can go with Momma into town when she mails her letter to Sally, and then go to the bank," once again speaking out loud but to no one in particular.

"I will tell Momma that I want to go see my friend, Molly, who lives on the outskirts of town," she whispered out loud, but not so loud that her mother could hear. She hadn't seen Molly for some time and thought it would be a good excuse to get Tilly to bring her with. Sarah thought some more about her plan, and she stopped crying and began to formulate her plan. She began to feel pretty proud of herself and thought that perhaps she could help find a way to stay. As she thought more about it, she became tired and as the sky was beginning to get dark, she decided to lay down for a while and just let her eyes have a rest. It had been a long day, and if her plan was going to work, she would need all her energy, and her ingenuity!

Section Seven

Joshua Finds a Way

"C'mon Joshua", yelled Mr. Potts. "Stop daydreamin' and get down here." "We can't wait all day to unload that wagon. It's getting near nightfall and I'm a mite hungry and don't want to miss my supper."

Joshua shook himself a bit, realized that he had been staring a bit too long, at what, he wasn't sure, and jumped down from the porch and ran over to the wagon. Truth be known, he hated lifting those heavy sacks of cotton, and then having to stack them in the barn, five sacks high along the north side of the barn. T "At least I don't have to take care of you critters anymore," Joshua said to the pigs and horses, all lined up on that south side of the barn, each group of animals having its own stall. Because he was a strong boy for his age, he was given the heavier work to do. The other, younger slave children were now in charge of those animals, feeding them, washing them, and making sure they didn't escape from the barn when them gates were open.

Joshua remembered the time when he was younger, and he was in charge of the animals' feeding. One time he forgot to close the gate to the pig pen and two of Mr. Andrews' prized sows got loose, and ran out of the barn. Before Joshua could catch them, one had got itself tangled in the barbed wire that was a layin' on the ground near the fence. Well, that sow screamed and tried to free itself from the barbed wire, but as it did, it got even more tangled. Mr. Potts had heard the screaming as well and he ran over with his whip, gave Joshua a sharp "thack" across his back and yelled: "Joshua, if anything happens to that sow, you will surely pay the price."

Joshua then jumped on the back of the sow and with the clippers lying next to the fence, clipped the barbed wire off that sow and then shooed it back into the barn.

Luckily, the sow was not too badly injured; just a few cuts where the barbed wire had cut a bit into its hide. "Before Mr. Andrews sees that sow, Joshua, you had better get it cleaned off and take care of those cuts," Mr. Potts instructed. Mr. Potts continued: "Joshua, I am real tired of having to look after all you people, day in and day out, and especially the likes of you. I am going to teach you a lesson you surely will not forget."

He then raised his whip again as if to strike Joshua, but before he could do so, he heard Mattie, Joshua's mother screaming: "Don't you whip that boy again. What he did or didn't do don't warrant his being whipped like some dumb animal. Besides, he is just a little one, and doesn't really know how to take care of them sows."

Mr. Potts drew back his whip, surprised at the outburst from Joshua's mother and stood there, somewhat bewildered. He looked around and saw no one else was there. He could see both the hurt and fear in Joshua's eyes, and the anger in Mattie's, and the way she clenched her fists and he decided to draw back. He thought to himself that maybe this was not the best time to carry out his usual physical abuse on Joshua. He thought to himself how many years he had been on the Andrews plantation and all the whippings he had rendered to countless numbers of slaves, old and young, and said to Joshua's mother, and to Joshua, looking straight at them,

"Next time, IF there is a next time, and there better not be, he won't get off so easy." Mr. Potts' voice was reaching a screaming level as he held back his whip and faced Mattie and looked at Joshua. He said further: "you Slaves," speaking directly to Mattie, "have no right to speak to me that way. Why, you are no better than those farm animals and don't you ever speak to me in that tone again or you will never forget the day you tasted this here whip. Oh no, you will never forget ol' Tom Potts. I am letting you off easy this time, but no more." Mr. Potts then walked away, most likely to his small cabin to drink away his anger the rest of the afternoon.

Joshua recalled that incident as if it were yesterday, and he never could get over the sound of Mr. Potts' voice, or what he said or the look in his eyes, or the sinister glare on his face, or the sorrowful look on the face of his mother as she withdrew from Mr. Potts' sight, grabbing Joshua's hand and pulling him along with her back to their cabin.

But that was a long time ago, and now he had work to do, as much as he hated the thought of it. He saw Mr. Potts standing there, with that whip in his hand, all ready to gather it up and aim it at him. Joshua knew that no one could do the work he did, in as fast a time as he could. He also knew that as long as he continued to work so hard, Mr. Andrews would be pleased; he could avoid the anger of Mr. Potts, and most importantly, his momma would be safe from Mr. Potts' anger and his merciless carrying on. Sometimes he wished he knew where his poppa was so he could help out in these types of occasions. But he would have to put that off till another time; time was wasting and he didn't want to incur Mr. Potts' wrath.

Still, he began thinking of a plan; a plan to escape the plantation, a plan to take his momma and himself to safety. He had heard of slaves who had escaped from some neighboring plantations. What with the war going on and the owners having less control over their slaves on a daily basis, some were able to steal off in the dead of night, never to be seen or heard from again.

He had heard of rumors around the plantation of some kind of escape route up North. He had heard that not everyone in the South was in favor of slavery; in fact, he had heard of some white folk, both in the South and North, who offered supplies, safekeeping, and guidance to escaped slaves. He wanted to find out more about that.

Each Sunday, the slaves on his plantation were given time off from working the fields. They were able to gather together in their quarters and sing some spirituals and visit with each other. Joshua would hear stories of the past, and sometimes, new, secret stories about escapes. He was not a shy boy, and often stayed longer and listened to the stories when the other children had returned to their quarters. He moved closer and listened to the older men who would gather around to talk, and spin yarns to pass the time. He also heard them talk sometimes about something called the Underground Railroad and how the slaves used that railroad to escape to points up North. Well, as Joshua listened week after week, he learned that it wasn't a real railroad at all, but was more of a pathway that escaped slaves would travel to escape the South and the chains of slavery. No more than four or five at a time, they would secret themselves through trails that passed through the woods, staying off the main roads. They mostly traveled at night, to avoid passersby asking them about where they were going or to avoid the risk of being captured. Being captured was certainly a mighty dangerous thing. The captured slaves would often be beaten, and sent back to the South to their masters. Even worse, they might be sold off to unknown masters.

As they traveled, they would reach certain points that were identified as places of safety. They could be farms, houses, or other buildings usually marked in some code known only by the slaves. There might be candles or a lantern in a window, markings on the fence posts of houses, or even finely knitted quilts that hung out to be seen. There was even talk that these quilts had sayings on them, sayings that gave them inspiration and directions to follow. They would spend some time there, receive food and shelter, and then move on. People who helped them had to be very careful, secretive in fact, for what they were doing was against the law and if they were found out, they could suffer tremendously.

Joshua also heard about the legend of a woman who helped the slaves, a Ms. Harriet Tubman, known to the slaves as the "Moses of her people." Now Joshua knew his bible, and knew the story of how Moses had led his people out of Egypt, and he understood what this meant. He thought that he would like to meet Ms. Tubman, this Moses lady, some day and maybe travel with her, but that would be for another day.

One Sunday, Joshua could not wait any longer. He was so anxious to hear more, to find out the way, so he approached one of the older men, Mr. Washington (many of the slave men took the names of some of the founding fathers of the country as they really had no names of their own, except what was given to them by their owners.)

"Mr. Washington, I know you understand the ways. I was hoping to talk to you about that Underground Railroad."

Mr. Washington's eyes brightened as he looked down at Joshua, then looked around him and saw there was no one else present, and said," Joshua, never bring that up in public again. If Massa, or Mr. Potts, or any of the other overseers hears you talkin' 'bout that, you had better start sayin' your prayers boy." He moved closer to Joshua and continued, "Come here boy and sit down. What I am going to tell you now must not be repeated to anyone, not even your momma." Joshua moved closer, his hands and face sweating, aware that what he was about to hear could very well change his life.

Section Eight

Martin Understands

A s Martin was lying on his bed, and searching the skies for answers, he heard a loud noise coming from downstairs in the kitchen. He thought for a minute and wondered what it could be. He jumped up, put on his shoes and his britches and long shirt and headed to the stairs that led down to the kitchen. He had spent several years in his "attic" and appreciated the quietude and independence he enjoyed away from the rest of the house. He decorated his area with things that made him happy, including a photograph of his mother and he when he was very young. He would often go to his room and look at that photo and wonder what his life would have been like if his mother was still in his life. But that was not to be.

Before he could move any further though, he heard voices coming from the kitchen, loud, angry voices, one of which was his father's. "William," he heard his father speak out, "what kind of an idea is that? Do you know what would happen to our foundry, to our very existence, if this leaked out to others?" William responded, "I know Samuel, but we can't keep up this charade any longer. I can't keep making up excuses every Sunday night to my wife about where I am going. I think that by now, she probably imagines me going down to town and doing some pretty raucous things, and god knows whom with. We must start making plans."

Samuel and William continued their conversation, although now in a much quieter tone, so low that Martin could no longer hear them. He inched down the stairs to get a closer position, possibly to hear better, but as he stepped on the last stair, the one that was supposed to be fixed last week because of the loose nails, it squeaked and both men turned as they heard the noise and looked at the stairway. There stood Martin, looking perplexed and a bit worried after being caught, kind of like how he felt when as a youngster, his mother found him one morning in the kitchen with his hand in the cookie jar, trying to grab some of his mother's freshly made butter cookies. "Martin, what on earth are you doing?" Samuel asked him, as William was stuffing some papers back into his satchel. "Oh, nothing father, I heard a noise and came down to see what had happened."

Samuel looked at Martin, then at William, and then again at Martin and said, "Well, we were talking and Mr. Stark's satchel fell off the table after he had nudged it with his elbow. He went to pick it up and then knocked into the vase on the table and then it fell, too. It is late, and we are both getting tired and perhaps a little clumsy. That is what you heard, nothing more."

Now Martin could tell the difference between a satchel or a vase falling to the ground and the sound of what seemed like a fist banging on the table, but he didn't say anything to his father, or to Mr. Stark. He knew that this was not the time to get more involved in their conversation. "Alright then, I reckon I will head back upstairs. It is getting late and there is a lot of work to do in the morning." So, Martin realizing it was time to depart, said, "Good night father, good night Mr. Stark."

Both men nodded to Martin and he followed the same path upstairs that he had used to come down, this time not as cautiously. He got back into bed after taking off his britches and his shoes and laying them on the chair next to his bed. He would have to get them back on first thing in the morning.

"Now see what you did, Samuel," Mr. Stark whispered. "Now your own son may know something. We have to be extremely careful if our plan is going to work."

"I know, I know," Samuel said. "I think this is the week that we make our move. It has been in the planning stages long enough. You get a hold of the others, and meet me tomorrow at the foundry office. I will advise my staff that we are meeting about the plan for a new postal office in town. You needn't worry them about our plan. Now, off with you. Go home to that pretty wife of yours and give my respects." "Surely will, Samuel," said Mr. Stark. "You take care and make sure that son of yours doesn't get wind of this. He is mighty crafty you know." "Yes, I am aware of that," Samuel said in a somewhat joking manner. "He does take after his mother you know." "Yes," William countered, "and his father too." With that, Mr. Stark got up and with his satchel in hand, walked out the door without looking back.

A few minutes later, Samuel yelled up the stairs, "Martin, would you come back down here? I need to talk to you." Martin was just beginning to nod off, beginning to dream how things used to be back before the War started, before his mother passed away from that consumption and he was startled to hear his father's voice. "Sure, Father, be right down," he yelled out. Samuel was still at the table and as Martin came once again down the stairs, and approached, he said to Martin, "Go get yourself a glass of milk and some of those cookies that I picked up in town. Actually, get me a glass of milk too. It has been a long time since we shared milk and cookies together, hasn't it?" Martin quickly obliged, and put the cookies and milk on the table, wondering why his father had all of a sudden changed his mood but also looking forward to the taste of those cookies. He could remember the times when his mother would make cookies to kind of soothe the evening and he looked forward to the taste of those warm, moist cookies.

"Martin, I know I haven't been spending much time with you lately, and I have been rather brusque with you, and with the others around the foundry. I have been under a lot of stress with the production for the war and the loss of so many workers who thought it their role to join up with the army and take part in this war and thought that now that you are sixteen, almost a man, that you should be aware of what is going on."

Martin began to get nervous; he could feel the uneasiness in his neck and arms as he sat still, listening to his father, and found it hard to continue making eye contact. "Martin, these meetings that have been going on around here lately, do you know what they have been about?" "Why no, sir," Martin responded.

"Well there is a plan afoot, which most likely will start next week, to provide safe havens and pathways for blacks to travel north to safety in Canada. This has been going on for several years, in various parts of the country, and now we are planning to assist those poor wretched souls to escape their miserable conditions. Martin, have you heard of the Underground Railroad?" Martin thought about it for a minute and knew that he did hear something about it a while back, but did not really know what is was all about. He heard some men in the foundry talking one afternoon, and briefly heard them talking about the war again, and how some of the blacks were able to escape from the plantations and farms in the South and head up North. That was about all he heard.

"I did hear some talk about that railroad, Father," Martin responded. "I would like to hear more though, and what this plan is all about." Samuel thought again of his wife, and how inquisitive she had always been and now understood why she always said that Martin was definitely her son, there could be no mistake!

"Well, some of the men in town have agreed that since we cannot fight in this war personally, we can still help in our own way." A number of us have offered to provide safe places for some runaways so they have a chance to get away. We have heard how this has worked down South, in Philadelphia and Boston and even in New York City, and figured why not here in on the banks of the Somerset River."

"Now, this is no easy task, as there are still slave hunters out there looking for runaways to take back to their masters. We have also heard how these slave hunters, as nasty and as mean as men could be, were also kidnapping free blacks, like the men you know in town, and selling and then secreting them to southern slave owners. You are probably not aware of the existence of the law that says that they can do that. It is called the Fugitive Slave Act. Most men I have talked to about this horrible law disagree with it, and often ignore it when asked about it, but it is still the law of the land. That is the awful truth, and even though it looks like the North is winning this war, it is definitely not over with, and many a slave, as well as free blacks, are being arrested or caught and sent back to the South, to be given back to the plantation owners.

Martin was having some difficulty digesting all this information, and at the same time, was trying not to jam up his mind thinking about what role HE could play in the war. "Father, I am not afraid and if I can help, well, I surely would be glad to in any way that I could." "Splendid, Martin." "But for now, I would like for you to just keep this thing quiet; don't tell any of your friends, or anyone in town. If this were to leak out, not only could word spread and quite possibly end our plan, but we could get in a heap of trouble."

Passed in 1850, the Fugitive Slave Act provided that any slave captured in the North, or anywhere one might be found, could be detained and returned to his master, no matter where he was found. Unfortunately, many free blacks were also pulled into this as well. Anyone found with such "contraband" as they were called, could be fined or thrown into jail. Although Mr. Lincoln was not in favor of this law, and made it well known to others, it was still in effect.

Martin was by now getting real tired and said, "Father, would it be alright for me to go back upstairs? I am just about ready to fall off this chair and if I don't get some sleep, I won't be worth anything tomorrow." "Sure son, but remember what I said. This is between you and me." With that, Mr. Wickham gave

Martin a hug and a pat on the rear. Martin turned and climbed back up the stairway, and hopped into his bed, not bothering to take off his clothes. He just stared out his window again, but this time, did not concern himself with the sky or the order of the planets or the stars. Nor did he think about the past. Knowing what he knew from his conversation with his father was enough, for now.

Section Nine

Abigail's Discovery

A s Abigail and Rachel "marched" down 16th street, avoiding all the debris that was still in the mud filled street, not far from her house, they talked about any number of things, not the least of which was the group of well-dressed women who were hovering near the corner they were approaching. "I wonder what all the hub bub is about," said Rachel. "I have no idea," Abigail responded, "let's get closer and see what is going on." Both girls hurried at first, but then slowed down. They didn't want the women to be startled by their approach, or question why they were there. As they got closer, they stopped and pretended to be speaking to each other. They heard one woman say: "Now girls, this can't go any further than here. If we are to help in any way, we have to be careful."

Abigail and Rachel looked at each other, not knowing what the women were talking about, but both girls wanted to hear more. They pretended to be pulling on their umbrellas as if they couldn't open them up, and then were straightening their skirts, brushing off some of the debris that they had picked up as they walked down the street. In doing so, however, they were close enough to the women to hear more.

"If I give you this Elizabeth, you have to make sure that it gets to Colonel Whiteside as soon as possible. You can't let anyone know what you are doing, or where you are going." "I know, I KNOW," said Elizabeth, as she took the notepaper from one of the ladies and put it in the folds of her dress. Abigail noticed that the skirts for women were billowy and contained many folds in them. Some were light blue in color, others were yellow and white and there was even one that was a light crimson. They all were wearing the latest fashionable bonnets, which effectively covered their entire heads and hairdos. "I have done this before," continued Elizabeth. "And, I know the best way to get out of Washington without being questioned. Just over the bridge there is a sentry who is familiar with our family; he always finds time to say hello and we chat a bit as I think he has taken a fancy to me. He has no idea what we are doing. He always asks me about the latest books I have read, or what is playing at Ford's Theatre. Our family just loves to go to Ford's Theatre."

"Good, then you had better go. Time is of the essence and the Colonel should have this information no later than tomorrow noon. The troops are gathering quickly and they want to move onto Washington soon," said Mrs. Greenhow, the oldest of the women, who seemed to act like the leader of the group. "I am getting a little tired of having to make sure everyone knows what they are doing," she continued. Then the women began walking away while still chatting among themselves.

"What is that all about?" questioned Rachel. "Beats me," said Abigail, as the girls continued walking away from the women.

"But I do know one of those women, the older one, the one doing most of the talking," Abigail replied. "I have seen her at our house from time to time, and on the street as well. She is a widow but I know she knows my father and some of the men he works with." "I will ask my father about her when I get home." "Alright," said Rachel, as she jumped over a puddle on the street.

"See if YOU can jump that puddle without getting wet, said Rachel." Although Abigail could not stop thinking about the women, and their conversation, she could not pass up a game of jump the puddle, so with her hands on her skirts, and the umbrella under her arm, she jumped and just made the outside edge of the puddle, as her heel made the tiniest of splashes at the very edge of the puddle. Just as she landed, she turned her head and saw Robert, coming down the street, bag in hand.

"Rachel, there's Robert. Let's go surprise him." With that, both girls began running down the street, trying to avoid the puddles and debris strewn all around, forgetting for the time being what they had just witnessed. "Robert, Robert, we see you," they both said in unison. With that, Robert turned, hoping that these girls suspected nothing about his being here. Good, he said to himself. He seemed satisfied that the secret of his presence was secure.

"Why girls, what could you two be doing now? Up to no good I bet?" "Well, we could ask the same of you Robert," said Abigail, as she stood with her hands on her hips, her head kicked back and her chin up. She loved to tease Robert and he knew it and accepted it. Although she wasn't his kin, she was the next best thing, and he did have fun toying with her and Rachel.

Remembering what she had just witnessed, Abigail asked Robert, "Robert, do you know a Colonel Whiteside?" Robert took on a serious look and said: "Now, why would you ask me that Abigail?" "No special reason, other than we heard some ladies mention his name just a bit ago."

Now Robert was educated not only in reading and writing, but also in the progress of the war, and knew enough of the happenings to have heard of Colonel Whiteside, the onetime Union officer who after the war started, gave up his command and joined the Army of Northern Virginia, the place of his birth. He and many other graduates of West Point, the Union military academy, had decided to return to their homes and join the forces of the South when the War started. Indeed, even Robert E. Lee, a former graduate of West Point, and a native son of Virginia, after being offered a position in the Union army based upon his extensive military skills, had declined, and joined the southern forces. He was now the Commander of the Army of Northern Virginia. His former estate near Washington was confiscated by the Union, an estate that had been in the Lee family for many years.

Robert looked at Abigail and said, not to worry her: "I am not sure. But I will find out for you. Now you two get along and have some fun, but Abigail, I expect you to be home in time for supper. See this here bag? I have to get some provisions for supper and you had better be home in time. I plan on making a right tasty meal today." "All right, Robert," Abigail said with a slight air of defiance. "I will be home in plenty of time. Bye." "Yes, goodbye Robert," Rachel added. Robert waved as both girls took off, but as they did so, he thought about Colonel

Whiteside and what the girls meant by their question. What did they really hear? Were they holding something back? He thought he should probably go back to the Handy house as soon as he could and let Mrs. Handy know of his meeting up with the girls, and their inquiry. He was sure she would be interested.

Meanwhile, Abigail and Rachel continued on their journey downtown. Since the rain had stopped, there were so many people out and about, they just liked to watch the goings on. Buggies filled with finely dressed ladies passed them by. Their drivers sat tall and straight in their seats, not paying attention to the conversations going on behind them, or so the ladies thought! "Rachel, what do you think those ladies we saw earlier were talking about? I am just dying to know," said Abigail. "Now, Abby (that was what Rachel had always called her) you had better mind your own business. You know how that nose of yours can get you in trouble." "I know, Rachel, but I can't help myself. You see, I often hear Mother and Father talking in the drawing room about people about town who can't always be trusted."

"What do you mean, Abby?" Rachel replied: "Well, I have heard them talking about spies here in Washington, you know, people who pretended to be a certain way but weren't." "What on earth do you mean, Abby," Rachel said in a highly curious tone. Abby replied: "There are people who you might think are loyal to the Union cause, like my father. But I have heard that some people who you might think are loyal, are really not. In fact, I have heard my mother talk about certain ladies who lived here in town and actually passed on secret information to the South." Now, Rachel was getting even more curious.

"Abby, you know so much about this spy business. Tell me more," Abby replied, "Remember those ladies we saw? Remember what they were wearing?" "Well sure I do, silly, Rachel offered. "They had on those long skirts with the folds in them. "Well, do you know what those folds are for?" responded Abby. "No, do you?" "Yes, I do. I have heard that ladies put secret coded messages in those folds, and then go to visit the soldiers across the bridge. Because they are considered proper ladies, they are not even searched, like some of the men are. I have even heard that one of the ladies even keeps a small pistol in those folds, just in case of any trouble." "Heavens," said Rachel in a surprising manner, "now you are scaring me a bit."

"Oh, I don't mean nothing by it, Rachel. I have probably talked too much now anyway. Let's get going back to my house. Pretty soon Robert will be back with the groceries for dinner and we don't want to disappoint." "Are you asking me to stay for dinner?" questioned Rachel. "Of course I am, don't you always have dinner with us on Wednesdays?" "Now that you mention it, I forgot what day this was," said Rachel. "All this talk about spies made me forget. You are right; let's get back to your house."

Both girls turned and began their walk back, still holding the umbrellas that had been of no use except to clear their paths of some leaves and small branches every now and then. "My mother is so protective," Abby said to Rachel as they neared her house. "I wish she would let me be some times." "I know what you mean," Rachel replied in a knowing manner, "my mother treats me like I was a ten- year old, always asking me where I am going, and telling me what time to come home. And then she asks me where I have been, who I was with, and so on."

Section Ten

Sarah's Town Visit

Going to town was always a treat for Sarah. She liked living on the farm and that was for sure. Putting on her overalls, the old hand- me- downs that belonged to her mother, was how she dressed most of the time. No need to get dressed up just to do farm work. Her hair was always pulled back with a ribbon or a bow though, preferably blue or yellow for they were her favorite colors. But every once in a while, she also liked getting dressed in her finer clothes, hopping into the wagon with her mother and father, and taking the ride into town to go shopping, saying hello to her friends and seeing all the new things that were at Mr. Small's store. Why, he stocked everything from grain and meal, to some canned goods that could be stored for weeks before using, to the newest styles straight from Charleston. She would just walk down the aisles and stare at everything, wishing she could just take handfuls of goods back with her to the farm. Her mother would always have to caution her to be careful though; Mr. Small did not take too kindly to children in his store, even well-behaved children like Sarah, for they would bump into things, not on purpose of course, but in a way that caused him to have to move around, rearrange things, and restock what he had spent his valuable time doing.

On this particular morning however, Sarah was not thinking about the store; her mind was preoccupied with thinking about how she was going to talk to Mr. Edmonds, the bank manager. She woke up early and even before she got dressed, she was planning her strategy. She would tell Mr. Edmonds how well the crops looked so early in the season (she didn't mind stretching the truth a bit) and how they were expected to bring in a sizeable harvest. Surely, after the sale of their crops, they would have enough money to not only pay what was owed to the bank, but have something left over for her mother and her to visit Mr. Small's store, to stock up on what was needed at home, and maybe even buy a new dress!

This time, however, her father was not with them, and hadn't been for a while, so she had to accept that her mother and her would be alone in the wagon. As they approached town, she did notice how few people were there and had forgotten how quiet things were. As many of the townsmen had gone off to war, there was not much commotion in the streets, or around the stores, so they were able to make their way from the farm pretty quickly. But she had to keep her mission secret; she did not want her mother to even have a hint about her plan to go to the bank. Her mother was going to mail her letter to her cousin and look around at Mr. Small's store, even though she wasn't able to purchase anything today. And besides, she was supposed to go "visit" her friend Molly.

"Momma," Sarah announced as they got to town, "you can drop me off here. Molly lives just down the street and I can find my own way." "If you wish," her mother said. "I will meet you back here at 11:00. Don't be late, as we have to get back to the farm." "Alright Momma," Sarah said happily, but also with some caution, for if her mother knew she was going to the bank, and not to Molly's house, she would certainly be upset and would most likely spoil her plans.

As Sarah approached the bank, she began to feel nervous; she could feel the moisture develop on her forehead and under her arms, and she thought about turning around. "What am I going to do?" she thought to herself. Even though she had been thinking about this all morning, she still wasn't sure exactly what she would say to Mr. Edmonds. As she walked into the bank, she saw where Mr. Edmonds was sitting, with his large desk, filled with paperwork, his high-backed chair and his very important looking suit of clothes that befit his position. As Sarah approached his desk, (there wasn't any receptionist or secretary to block her path) she could see the sweat beading up on his bald head even this early in the morning and noticed how he would take his handkerchief and wipe his head, then his glasses, then his head again. She wondered how uncomfortable he must be to work there in the heat of the day with that suit and all. There were not many people in the bank this morning, and she felt a mixture of confidence and nervousness, something she was not really used to.

She walked up to him and as he looked up at her, she said, "hello Mr. Edmonds, my name is Sarah Andrews." "Well good morning, Sarah, nice to meet you," he replied with a smile on his face, and he put out his hand to offer a handshake. The name Andrews sounded familiar to him, although he couldn't place it right away. Sarah shook his hand and thought that he seemed very nice. Maybe this won't be so bad after all she thought to herself.

"What can I do for you Sarah?" he offered, and invited Sarah to have a seat in the big, red, cushioned chair that faced his desk. As she sat down, she said, "Mr. Edmonds, my daddy has not come back from the war yet, and we kind of fell behind in our payments to the bank. My momma said that we were close to eviction." Mr. Edmonds looked intently at Sarah, as he now was reminded of the situation with the Andrews farm; he had been the one that sent the notice for the eviction. "Well now, Sarah," he commented, "tell me how old you are." Sarah replied with conviction, "I am almost fourteen years old, sir."

Sarah continued: "My mother said that we should have a pretty big harvest this fall. That means that we will be able to repay the bank all that we owe and then some. I was hoping that you could call off this eviction thing so we could keep the farm. When my daddy comes back from the war, he will be able to go back to farming and we can all stay together." Mr. Edmonds could see the hope in Sarah's face, although he knew that there was no way that they could call off their eviction; they were simply too far behind in their payments. He didn't want to disappoint her, yet he had to be as real as he could be with her at the same time. "Sarah, I really appreciate your coming here and speaking with me. And, I would really like to help you and your family out," offered Mr. Edmonds. Sarah was listening carefully, but she could tell from the look on Mr. Edmonds' face and from the tone of his voice that this was not going to be good news.

"Sarah, let me explain something." Mr. Edmonds got up from his chair and came around his desk and sat next to Sarah, pulling up his chair pretty close to her. "Our bank here is a business and, as businesses go, a pretty good one. Now, because we are a business, we have to be careful where our investments go. We have helped out a lot of farmers around here over the years, and your family is one of the many families who do business with us. Some have been able to pay their bills to us, but not all. We have extended time for them to make their payments. Your family's payments are way behind, and I am afraid that this bank cannot give you more time. I have to answer to the other owners of the bank, who have their own bills to pay. I am not sure you understand all of this, you are very young." He could see the fear building up in Sarah's eyes and on her face, and didn't want to make her more upset than she already was. "Sarah, I will tell you what. I cannot promise you anything, but I will look back at our records, and if there is any way that I can help, I will."

Mr. Edmonds knew the position of the bank, but didn't have the heart to tell Sarah that there was no possible way the bank could recall the eviction, so he offered her the possibility of help. He too was upset, as he has had this same type of conversation with a number of farmers recently. Ever since the war started, the bank had lost business, payments were behind, and his job as manager meant he had to keep the bank afloat. If that meant upsetting some people, like Sarah, well, he couldn't help it. It didn't make him feel any better, but it helped justify his business decisions.

"Thank you, Mr. Edmonds," Sarah said as she got up to leave. "I do hope you can help. One more thing," she said as she turned back to Mr. Edmonds, "could you not mention to my mother that I was here!" "Of course, Sarah. This will be our little secret." Mr. Edmonds whispered. "Now, go off and have a nice day. Here, take this peppermint stick with you. I know kids love peppermint sticks and they are pretty hard to come by these days. Good bye." "Good bye Mr. Edmonds," and Sarah left the bank, still with a bit of hope that their farm could be saved as she tucked that peppermint stick into her pocket, saving it for a time when her mother wouldn't see it and then have to say where she got it.

As Sarah walked out, Mr. Edmonds thought to himself about the farm failures that the bank had experienced over the last two years. As he put his hands in his pockets and began twirling his watch chain in his fingers, he looked out the window and saw how quiet the street was. He said out loud but to no one in particular, "This war has produced nothing but misery and despair around here. I do hope that President Davis (referring to Jefferson Davis, the President of the Confederacy) knows what he is doing. We have been at war for two years now, and I don't know how much longer we can hold out." He shook his head and walked back to his desk to see what other bad news had come to him during the course of the morning, at just about the time that Sarah met up with her mother in front of Mr. Small's store.

Section Eleven

Joshua Makes a Decision

Joshua was always told to respect his elders, as his mother had told him, over and over again, and when he addressed Mr. Washington, he would always be respectful calling him Mr. Washington. He didn't know how Mr. Washington had come to the plantation. He surely must be real old, as evidenced by his grizzled gray hair and stooped over way of standing. Joshua only knew that he had been there a long time and that the slaves on the plantation often would go to him with questions or seeking his advice. He had listened over time as Mr. Washington would tell the others to behave and don't ask so many questions, lest they receive beatings like he had received over the years, especially when he was a young buck with a lot of courage, and a disdain for his master's rule, with a voice to match.

"See here boy," Mr. Washington said as he pulled up his soiled and torn cloth shirt, over his back and turned to Joshua. "See these marks on my back? Why, these marks, these scars, I got them many years ago when my master became impatient with me. I made the mistake of talking back, you know, out of turn, and said some things that I now wish that I hadn't. Back in those days, and which still happens to some young blacks now, I was tied to the tree, my shirt was taken off, and while the other slaves looked on, my master had the overseer (for my master could not muster up the courage to do it himself) take the whip and start to beat me with it. I wasn't able to move, and I greeted each crack of the whip with an anger that you cannot even imagine. I was young and strong, and the whippings surely hurt. But I wouldn't let my master know how bad it hurt and I would just stand there as long as I could, staying silent on the outside but feeling the fire in my belly and in my head burning like a raging bonfire.

After some twenty blows, I could feel the skin on my back beginning to break, and could see the blood dripping down around me. I heard crying from the other slaves, and even my master's woman was saying, enough Jeremy. That is enough. You are going to kill him unless you stop.

"You see, Joshua, whipping a slave back in those days, and even now, is nothing to the slave owners. We are just property and are treated as if we have no rights, no thoughts or feelings of our own. Mr. Jeremy finally stopped and the other slaves helped me up and carried me back to my cabin. They cleaned up my back as best they could, and put some salve on it and laid me on my stomach. It was days before I could even walk again, and even then, I could feel the pain in my back, the same pain I feel every day when I think about it. Sure, the skin healed, but the memories are still right here in my head, along with the pain."

As Mr. Washington continued, Joshua just sat there thinking about his own future. Would he be getting beatings as well? Then Mr. Washington spoke up again, but this time a little more quietly: "I have heard a lot about how slaves are treated all across the South, Joshua. I even heard about how, several years ago, our own Supreme Court in Washington, had decided that we were just property. You were too young to know, but in fact, the Supreme Court, the highest court in this here land, had heard the case of Mr. Dred Scott, who at one time was a slave, and had sued the court for his freedom.

After many years of fighting, the Supreme Court decided that he did not have any right to even be in court; that he was just property and could be treated any way his master wanted.

Now, I am telling you this to help you understand what has been going on, and why you have to make a break for it. You are young, you are brave and even a bit aggressive; I could tell from the way you talk about Mr. Potts. I don't want to see you get in any trouble and I surely don't want you to have these scars on your back, or maybe worse."

Joshua was taking this all in; he wasn't too good at book learnin' but he sure knew what those scars meant. "I ain't never gonna let anyone do that to me," he whispered to himself. "I have to get out of here." He thanked Mr. Washington for his advice, and after Mr. Washington told him more about the Underground Railroad, he ran back towards his cabin and began to think about his future and what plans he had to make. He knew he couldn't tell his mother; she would just worry and try to convince him to stay. But then he thought out loud, "What about momma? What would happen to her if I left? "He knew that Mr. Potts would be mighty angry and would probably take his anger out on his mother. He didn't want this to happen, but at the same time, he couldn't keep staying on the plantation knowing all that he knew with no future for him other than to be a slave the rest of his life.

As he was running back to the cabin, he avoided the others on the plantation and looked around for Mr. Potts, but couldn't see him. He suddenly began to feel a sense like something was wrong. He slowed down his pace and began walking, still looking around for Mr. Potts, and though he did not see him, his uneasiness began to grow. He finally got to his cabin and it seemed unusually quiet; he slowed down and looked around but no one was there. He walked through the doorway and could smell something, a foul smell that was all too familiar to him. He had smelled this same smell before, after some beatings on the plantation. He started shaking; he was scared and could not see his mother.

He turned to the corner of the room where she usually sat in the late afternoon, to take a break from the day's work. She liked to sit there and look out the window, watching as the day passed into night.

As he moved into the cabin, he saw that she was indeed sitting there in her chair, but she was kind of stooped over and wasn't moving. He ran up to the chair and saw some drops of blood on the floor under the chair. He didn't want to look, but he had to. He turned the chair around and saw his mother slumped forward, her hands in her lap, the top of her head matted with blood and dirt and she wasn't moving. "Momma, Momma, wake up!" he shouted, hoping for the best but knowing in his heart that she was not alright. "Momma, are you ok?" he said as he shook her shoulder.

But she did not respond; she didn't move. "Momma, talk to me," he shouted. He looked at her and she had this queer look on her face. He couldn't understand what was going on. As he shook her, her head dropped even more and as he was shaking her, he cried out loud: "She is gone." He sat down, still holding her hand, and as tears started to fall from his eyes, he wiped the tears away, and began to try to figure what had happened. Suddenly, Peter, one of the slaves on the plantation who Joshua would often spend time with ran through the door and exclaimed, "Joshua, I was hoping you would come back, but not at this time, not now."

"Peter, what happened," Joshua yelled out. Peter stood there for a moment, not sure what to say to Joshua or how to explain what had happened. He looked over to Joshua's mother and back to Joshua and said: "Joshua, Mr. Potts heard that you went to talk to the other men, and especially Mr. Washington, and he got all upset and came down to your momma's cabin. He had been drinking some of that corn whiskey that he keeps in his quarters and was most likely beyond reasoning. He was yelling at her as if she had done some terrible deed, and then he began to beat her with that whip a' his. I could hear her cry out but I couldn't get there in time. When I did, she was already, well, she was in her favorite chair and just sittin' there. Mr. Potts was pushing his way out of the house knocking over the furniture and just took off. I tried to wake her up but she wouldn't move. I didn't know where you were, and neither did the others. I didn't want you to see her like this."

Joshua held back his tears, stood up straight as he could and focused on Peter, but his thoughts went to visions of Mr.

Potts beating his mother, with that look on Mr. Potts' greasy face he was all too familiar with. Oh, how his mother must have suffered, and that awful pain from that whip. His tears evaporated, and his mind shifted to Mr. Potts and that whip of his. "Peter, I have to find Potts," Joshua said.

"Joshua, now you wait a bit; old Potts took off with his bottle and is stored up in his cabin. You know how he gets." Joshua didn't care; he could only think about his mother and what she must have gone through because of him, because of his mixin' with the others. His sadness turned to anger and then rage, and he felt his blood getting hotter and he knew what he had to do.

"Peter, I have to find him. I have to do something. Please take care of my mother for me. Make her comfortable." With that, Joshua picked himself up and ran out the doorway. Peter knew what Joshua meant, and he also knew that he probably would not see Joshua again after this day. He just had that feeling. He also knew that things around the plantation would never be the same again. He turned and looked at Joshua's mother again, and worried about Joshua, with his anger and all, and what he might do.

Section Twelve

Martin Hears the Call

Martin was relieved when his father gave him the day off from work. He hadn't slept too well, with all the happenings the night before, so when his father asked him to go into town, he gratefully agreed. "Martin, I want you to stop in to see Mr. Stark and give him my regards before you go to the tailor. He left in quite a huff last night and I want to make sure that all is well. When you get to the tailor, see if my new suit is ready. I need to wear it Saturday night and it was promised to me for last week. There is so much going on right now that I can't get away."

Martin responded quickly, thinking that now he would have a chance to look around town a bit; he hadn't been there for a while and he heard there were some Army recruiters down on 4th Street, advertising for new recruits. "Father, would it be alright if I visited some friends in town as well? I haven't seen them for quite a while." "That will be alright, so long as you get back by dinner," his father said. "While you are there, why don't you pick up some of that licorice that Mr. Hammond keeps behind the counter in his grocery store? You know, the black and red kind that you used to like so much!" Martin thought for a minute and was surprised when his father mentioned the licorice; he hadn't had any licorice in a long time, and the thought of having some again sounded delightful.

"I will saddle up the mare; she certainly needs the exercise," Martin yelled to his father as he ran out the front door. He ran to the barn and thought that this would be a grand day as he put the blanket and saddle carefully up on the mare, cinched it up, and got his hat and jacket and then waved to his father who was standing in the doorway of the house.

As he came to town, he saw a crowd gathering around the post office and decided to stop there first to see what was going on before going to see Mr. Stark or the tailor.

"Come now lads. You don't want to miss out on the action," shouted the soldier who was standing on the porch of the post office. "Mr. Lincoln has those Rebs on the run and we need some additional men to make sure this war ends right now." Martin looked around and saw some men that he recognized, but no real close friends. He dismounted and began walking towards the soldier, holding the reins of the mare in his hand, not sure what he thought about all this. As he approached the porch, he saw a poster on the wall of the post office that the soldier was pointing to. It read:

RECRUITS WANTED: FIRST REGIMENT, NATIONAL VOLUNTEERS. CRACK REGIMENT; BOYS, DON'T BE DRAFTED. GET YOUR BOUNTY: $50 FROM THE STATE! $40 FROM THE UNITED STATES! $90 IN ADVANCE; EXPERIENCED OFFICERS FROM THE FIELD.

NOW IS YOUR LAST CHANCE FOR THE BOUNTY!

RECRUITING OFFICE: CAMP WASHINGTON, STATEN ISLAND; AT ONCE!

RAYMOND D. HAUFLER, RECRUITING OFFICER.

He tied up his horse to the nearest hitching post and after looking around again to see if anyone recognized him, he walked up to the soldier who was talking to some men on the porch and said, in his deepest voice, "Excuse me sir, but where are these recruits going to go?" "Son, the lucky lads who join up will be shipped down near Washington. Mr. Lincoln expects for the Army of the Potomac to be increasing in size. General Lee seems to be inching closer with his troops and we don't have a moment to lose. Might you be interested in joining up? We could use a strong looking lad like you. And you sound like a bright one too. You could probably move up in the ranks real, quick like."

Martin could not believe his ears. Did this soldier really want him? He knew he was big for his age, and with all the hauling and lifting he had been doing at the foundry, he was pretty well built up, but to enlist? He thought of his friend, Billy Bonham, and wondered where he was now. "Mister," he began, but was immediately stopped by the soldier, "you call me sir, son, and the name is Sgt. Hull, Thomas Hull, of the Second Regiment, New York 5th Army. Whenever you address a soldier in uniform, you always say sir, you understand?" Martin felt a bit ashamed; he should have known better, he thought, but then again, how could he? "I am sorry, sir, I, I mean Sgt. Hull." "What is your name son?" Sgt. Hull inquired. "Martin, sir, Martin Wickham," Martin replied. "And young Mr. Wickham, I will ask you again, are you interested in joining up?" "I am thinking about it sir," Martin said unconvincingly.

He had been thinking more and more about it of late, and especially since he heard about the Underground Railroad and the plans his father had been making. He wanted to do his fair share as well. Still, he was only sixteen (although he looked older) but he also knew how to handle a rifle and ride a horse real well.

"How long are you going to be in town, sir?" Martin asked. Sgt. Hull responded," I will be here until tomorrow; then I have to go down to Morristown and do some recruiting there as well. I will be leaving about noon, so if you decide to join up, make sure you stop here before noon, otherwise you will lose your chance." By the way, can you read and write?" Martin thought for a moment how odd a request that was for he was way up on his schooling, but he had heard that many of the soldiers, on both sides, could neither read nor write. "I sure can," Martin replied.

And with that, Sgt. Hull shook Martin's hand and went inside the post office to do his business. Martin stepped down from the porch, unhitched his horse and got back up into the saddle. He knew he still had to see Mr. Stark and go to the tailor, for he had promised his father he would do so. But he kept thinking about the poster he read, the look on the face of Sgt. Hull, the bounty they were paying, the excitement about really making a difference instead of just thinking about it…But what would his father say? Would he be agreeable? Probably not, not after the conversation they had yesterday. He would have to think long and hard; would this be the opportunity he had been hoping for? To escape the foundry, his way of life, the tedium of the foundry work? He loved and respected his father, but with his mother gone, and his father wrapped up in his business so, could he really do this? He could feel the tingling in his spine as he thought more and more about joining up.

After he stopped and paid his regards to Mr. Stark, who was very accommodating and who apologized for the scene the night before, he visited the tailor and picked up his father's suit. He then went over to the general store and purchased the licorice his father had mentioned and began riding back home. He was picturing himself in that new, blue uniform, with the gold buttons and gold sash around the waist, the one he had seen Sgt. Hull wearing, riding a fine horse and carrying a new government-issued carbine, surrounded by other soldiers, all there for a common purpose, to protect and preserve the Union. The thought of the excitement was so strong he could taste it. He envisioned himself riding into battle. Now as he rode, he could feel the sweat dripping off his forehead and in the palms of his hands as he thought more and more about what had just happened and what it meant.

By the time he got home, and after putting the mare into the barn, taking off her saddle and wiping her down, he had made up his mind. As he walked into the house with his father's suit, he placed it on the sofa in the great room. He called out for his father but did not get a response. He then climbed the stairs back to his room, looked around and said to no one in particular, "I will miss this room." He gathered up some of his things, packed them in the heavy canvas bag he used for carrying firewood into the house, laid back on his bed and thought how much his life has already changed since just last night. He no longer had to look at the stars and wonder. As he was falling asleep, he knew his decision was made.

Section Thirteen

Abigail and Robert
Talk Over Pie

A fter dinner, Abigail and Rachel gathered their plates and silverware and left the table and went into the kitchen to see Robert. Her parents stayed around the table and talked about the day's happenings in the Agriculture Department. "Mr. Lincoln wants me to take a trip down to a town called Gettysburg, Mr. Handy stated to his wife. "He seems to think that the country around that town is really ideal for growing crops and for cattle raising. We certainly could use some help in supplying our boys in the field, and Gettysburg just might be the answer." "But John, isn't that a bit dangerous?" Mrs. Handy replied.

"No dear," Mr. Handy offered. "I hear that Gettysburg is a pretty safe area; the Rebs are no way near there and have no real call to go there anyway. Maybe you and Abigail can come with me for a spell, just to get away from this town for a while."

Mr. Handy knew how Mrs. Handy and Abigail needed to get away from Washington, with all its noise and smells and sights of war. He had witnessed the soldiers around town and had seen their injuries. Boys no older than eighteen (and some even younger but with no formal recognition of age at the time of enlistment they were allowed to join nevertheless) were arriving daily. They had horrible wounds, too difficult to describe to his wife and daughter, and the numbers of returning soldiers increased daily. He was too old to fight, and was glad he had no son to enter the fray, but he still worried about what he saw.

He had heard Mr. Lincoln give his speech called the Emancipation Proclamation a short while ago, and as a northern born and bred man, knew that Mr. Lincoln believed in the right of the blacks to be free. He also knew that Mr. Lincoln, above all, wanted the Union to stay intact; that all the states that seceded should be brought back into the Union. That was the subject of many of his speeches, and with the Emancipation Proclamation being issued, he also was aware of how much hatred there was in the South for President Lincoln's opinions about slavery. He knew that the southern papers had printed articles that called Lincoln some nasty names, and how he was trying to destroy their way of life.

As Abigail and Rachel entered the kitchen, they put their dishes and silverware in the sink and looked over at Robert.

"Robert, now that I am older, I want to hear about how you came to work with us," said Abigail, as she and Rachel approached Robert as he was busy cleaning up all the pots and pans he used to make dinner. Wiping his hands on the towel that he grabbed from the sink, now wet from wiping down the dishes, Robert replied: "Now, why would you want to know that, young lady?" Robert became a bit uneasy and looked around to see if

Mr. or Mrs. Handy were near. Abigail had never addressed this with him before, and he wasn't sure if she was ready to hear the truth, or if the Handys really wanted Abigail to hear this. He also wondered to himself if he was ready to tell Abigail the truth. It had been a long time since Robert had left South Carolina and his family and just the thought of it saddened him. And yet, after all these years, he hadn't spoken a word about his escape from the plantation or about his beatings to anyone, and perhaps the time had come to say something. "Now I am going to take a seat here for a minute, girls. I'm a mite tired. It's been a long day." And as he sat, the girls looked at each other with a quizzical look in their eyes.

Robert thought to himself about those days, long ago, when he and his woman (she was not legally his wife as slaves were not allowed to marry at that time) were sold to another owner who was kind enough, but who had a mean and nasty overseer. As a younger man, Robert was quite outspoken about what he wanted, and angered many people, especially the overseer, who would confront Robert almost daily. At first, they were little things; a misplaced saddle, a broken plow, etc. But over time, as Robert grew angrier about the way the overseer treated his woman and remarked about his newborn son and the way he would be blamed and then beaten for anything that happened on the plantation, he made a plan. He thought that if he was going to survive, he would have to leave. He and his woman talked about it and they both cried and held each other but they both knew that he had to leave. That was the only way he would survive.

"Come on Robert." Abigail pulled on Robert's arm as he once again focused on her and her request. "Tell me what happened." Abigail could be persistent, but Robert thought it better not to say anything now; it just simply wasn't right to tell this young girl about his past. Besides, Mr. Handy most likely would not approve, so he said, "young lady, before I can say anything at all, you had better get some of that pie cut and brought out to your mother and father." Abigail could tell when Robert wanted to talk, and when he didn't, and by the look on his face right now, she didn't want to push the issue any further, not now. "Robert, you make the best pie in Washington, and probably in the whole world," Abigail exclaimed. Rachel shook her head in agreement, and Robert was relieved that the issue of his past was once again pushed aside. He also knew that he could not keep his secret much longer.

"Mother, Father, here is the most delicious smelling and probably the best tasting pie in all of Washington," Abigail said proudly as she carried that pie into the dining room, as Rachel followed with the whipped cream they had so carefully whipped up in the kitchen. It was Mr. Handy's favorite, and always seemed to put him in a good mood.

"Mother," (that was how Mr. Handy called Mrs. Handy when Abigail was around) what do you think about going to Gettysburg for a while?" Mrs. Handy thought a bit, and thought about the drudgery of Washington lately and since her husband knew of the progress of the war, and that he probably thought it was safe enough to go, responded: "If you think it is a good idea, then how can I resist?" "Fine then," said Mr. Handy. "I will make the necessary arrangements and let you know when it will be the best time to go." "I will have my staff look into accommodations and transportation. It shouldn't take too long. And of course, I will have to talk to Mr. Lincoln himself."

Mr. Handy was proud of his decision to accept Mr. Lincoln's suggestion and of his political relationship with Mr. Lincoln. He had come a long way from being raised as a poor boy in Pittsburgh, but through hard work and determination, the kind of determination he saw in his daughter, Abigail, life was better for him and his family now, better than ever before. He now saw others that were constantly on the streets, or in the office buildings. He would have something that he had not had since he left Pittsburgh; some time on his own with his family. He had an opportunity to take his wife and daughter away for a bit, to escape Washington and its uproar about the war, the nasty weather and crowds of soldiers, politicians, favor seekers and heard many good things about Gettysburg and wished to visit.

"Robert," Mr. Handy said as he walked into the kitchen. "We are going to take a little trip to Gettysburg soon, as soon as I can straighten things out and get my office in order, and I would like for you to come along with us. You are a part of this family and the time away will do you good as well." "Why, Mr. Handy, I don't know what to say," as Robert was once again drying his hands on the dishtowel next to the sink. "That is right kindly of you, and I do appreciate your graciousness, but I don't know about me traveling with a white family. I haven't been away from Washington in a long time." (He thought of those days on the plantation again.)

"Robert, you now are a free man, working for a member of Mr. Lincoln's cabinet, and you have every right to do so," Mr. Handy stated emphatically. "Besides, I need someone to help take care of that curmudgeon daughter of mine while I am busy." Robert looked at Mr. Handy and they both laughed, knowing the truth in Mr. Handy's statement. With that, Mr. Handy extended his hand to Robert. Robert took Mr. Handy's hand in his own, and began to shake it. As he did so, he could feel the tears welling up in his eyes. The thoughts of family once again entered his head.

Section Fourteen

Sarah's Move

I t had been several days, or maybe even a week, since Sarah and her mother visited town. Things around the farm were not any better; in fact, even their farmhands had slipped silently away, to find work elsewhere. There simply wasn't any more work for them to do and Sarah's mother couldn't afford to pay them anymore. They asked her if they could go and find other work. Sarah's mother could not say no; she knew the conditions on the farm and knew she couldn't afford to pay her farmhands any more wages. She agreed to give them their "papers," which in effect gave them their freedom to travel about and find another farm or plantation to work on.

Conditions elsewhere in the South were not much better either. Many of the smaller farmers had simply given up and let their farms go. The bigger plantations, although still workable, had to scale back as their ability to produce had been reduced greatly.

"Momma, have you heard from your cousin yet?" Sarah asked her mother one morning, as they were both in the chicken coop looking for eggs. "Why, as a matter of fact, I have Sarah. Just yesterday I got a letter from Sally." Tilly then pulled out a letter from her pocket and apologized to Sarah. "I'm sorry, baby. This just came and I forgot all about showing it to you. Sally said we were welcome to come and stay with her and her family. She said that she understood our predicament, and that there was plenty of room for us on her ranch land near Gettysburg, Pennsylvania. All we have to do is pack up some things and find a way to get up there. She would have offered to pay our way, but with the war on and everything, she just couldn't do it. But once we got up there, we could help her on the ranch. She said you would love it there. It wasn't quite as hot as it is here, and there were plenty of girls your age in and around town that you could meet."

Sarah almost burst with delight as she thought about the move, although she could not forget about her meeting with Mr. Edwards at the bank. "Momma, have you gotten any more word from the bank about the farm?" Sarah asked. "No dear, I have not. Why do you ask?" responded Tilly. Sarah thought it best not to mention her meeting with Mr. Edwards. She didn't want to anger her mother. "Oh, I don't know. I just was curious since we got that first notice from the bank. But Momma, what will happen to the farm if we leave?" Sarah inquired. "Well, I am sure that the animals will be taken care of by our neighbor, and the crops, well, the crops probably won't make it anyway," responded Tilly. They both looked at each other, each without something further to say, and Tilly thought it best to move on.

"Sarah, I think its best that we start collecting our things and determine what we really need if we are going to go. I need to make arrangements to find a way to get up to Gettysburg and the sooner we know what we are bringing, the faster we can go.

Things are not getting any better down here and we don't want to wait until it is too late." Tilly thought about all the changes that they would go through in order to leave and she shuddered so hard that her skirt wiggled back and forth like it had been picked at by the wind.

Tilly was concerned about Sarah and of course, about her husband. Although she had not heard from him in a long time, she was sure he was all right. She just had that feeling, kind of like when you are walking down a road and hit a fork in the road and try to decide which one to take. All of a sudden something inside makes you make a choice that you know is right and you do so, finding out later that it was the right choice. That's how she felt now about her husband returning. That made her more comfortable and she said to Sarah," Darling, you can take whichever of your things you'll need. Especially your stuffed doll, the one with the curls that you like so much." "Momma, of course I will take Melinda. She is my favorite," Sarah said with such excitement in her voice you would think she was getting a new doll for the first time.

"Ok then, you go off and do your chores and I will look around this old farm and see what we need to pack to take with us. I will let our neighbors know of our leaving too, which should be within the week. They can watch over the farm while we are away. And, if daddy comes back while we are gone, they can tell him that we went up North to visit my cousin Sally Mayberry. Now off with you."

As Sarah ran off, Tilly thought about this move. Was it the right thing to do? She still didn't know quite how they would get to Gettysburg; it was a long way off. "Tomorrow, I will check in town and see what we should do," she said to herself as she looked around the farm and its dry land, wilted crops and broken-down machinery. Yes, tomorrow will mark the beginning of our journey and only the good Lord will know what happens next.

Section Fifteen

Joshua Escapes

He knew where Mr. Potts was. He had often walked by the cabin where Mr. Potts would stay, all by himself, nursing his bottle of whatever spirit he could find. Each night, after all the work on the plantation had been done for the day, and all the equipment had been put away, Mr. Potts would return to his cabin, and most often would fall asleep in his chair after drinking himself into a stupor. He was not a happy man, in fact, he was downright miserable.

He had no family to speak of and even Mr. Andrews didn't care much for him. He only kept him on because he got the job done with the slaves. Sure, he was the overseer but in his heart, he knew that he was just a hired hand, to do the master's will when the master could not. Ever since he was a boy, Mr. Potts was made fun of; he was not strong, not big, except in his stomach, which was as bloated as a pig ready for slaughter. He was not very smart, never finished his schooling and was often the one who other kids he grew up with made fun of. That is probably why he became an overseer; to get back at those who were less fortunate than he was, the ones who could not fight back.

Joshua moved a little more quickly as he approached the cabin. His anger was overwhelming, as was his grief for his momma. He knew that Mr. Potts was responsible for her leaving this Earth and he knew he had to make amends, to get back at Mr. Potts and at everyone who had hurt his mother and him over these many years. As he approached Mr. Potts' cabin, he heard nothing except a loud snore, the snore of a man who had too much to drink and then nodded off. Still, he could not suppress his anger as he entered the doorway.

He saw Mr. Potts sitting in his reclining chair, a bottle in his hand and the nastiest smell he could remember in the air. He saw a whip against the doorway and knew what he had to do. He picked it up but as he did so, he tripped over a tear in the ragged red carpet on the floor that had been crumpled up and he fell against the table in front of Mr. Potts. As he did so, the noise woke up Mr. Potts, who wiped his mouth, cleared his eyes with his dirty sleeve, and shouted in his slurred, drunken drawl: "Hey boy, what are you doing here? What do you want?" Joshua began to speak but before he could do so, Mr. Potts slowly moved up out of his chair and saw the whip in Joshua's hand.

"Boy, what are you doing with that whip?" Potts shouted, trying to gain his balance. The drink had dulled his senses and made it hard for him to stand up straight. "You put that whip down and get yourself out of here, right now." Joshua could feel his hand grip the whip harder, knowing that one swing of that whip was all he needed, one swing to settle accounts. "Boy, I told you to put that whip down. By God, if you don't, I will make you forever remember me and what I am about to do to you. Your momma didn't listen to me and she suffered the consequences. Now, it is your turn.

Mr. Potts raised himself from the chair and began to move towards Joshua, but just as he did so, and just as Joshua was about to draw that whip back, Mr. Potts tripped over the leg of his chair and fell forward, hitting his head against the edge of the table that now held his bottle, and another that had been emptied earlier. He fell with a thud and Joshua could see the blood began to flow from his head. He just stood there, with the whip in his hand, watching. He thought about his mother. He thought about Mr. Potts, who lay there motionless, and as he saw the blood ooze from his head, he knew. He knew that Mr. Potts was gone. He didn't have to use the whip anymore; it was pointless now. There was nothing else he could do. As he stood there, he also realized that he might be blamed for what happened. He had to decide what to do.

He thought of his conversation with Mr. Washington and the Underground Railroad.

He only had one choice; to leave this plantation forever and find a new life. There was nothing more to keep him here. He dropped the whip on the floor and ran out the door. He didn't look back and knew that Mr. Potts got what was coming to him. Now he had to find the right path to take; to get away from this plantation.

He ran, and as he ran he thought of the conversations he had had with his mother. Those many nights when they would talk about her past, her family, his father and what might have happened to him. He didn't remember his father; he was sold off when Joshua was just a very little boy. His mother had told him he was a brave, strong man. He believed in what was right, and when the master realized how he might be a problem with the other slaves, he made a point of selling him off right away, lest he would cause a problem. Joshua thought about him; tried to imagine how he must have looked. His mother had told him of the terrible scar on the side of his face, a scar he had gotten from a beating long ago, way before Joshua was even born. Maybe someday, he thought, maybe someday I will find him. But for now, he had to run, run away and save himself. Find that Underground Railroad. Find that way up North. Find his way to freedom from the pain, the suffering and the thoughts of his mother.

He ran and continued running until he reached the fence that bordered the plantation. He only had one choice now; he jumped, cleared the fence, and with just the clothes on his back and the memories of what had happened, he made for the woods. But where was he to go? Now, it didn't matter. He just kept running until the exhaustion overtook him. He slowed down and when he realized how far he was from the plantation, he stopped. All he could see was forest; the low hanging oaks and bays, and the bramble bushes and broken branches. He heard nothing from behind him. No yelling or no dogs barking. Was he clear? Was he free? He didn't know. All he knew was that he was tired and hungry and thirsty.

He decided to stop a bit and rest. He leaned up against a tree and put his head back against the trunk of an old oak and thought about the day, about what he had seen and how his life was never going to be the same again. He wanted to stay awake and make a plan for his next move. As darkness set in, and the birds started with their familiar calls, he slowly drifted into a silence and peace that he had not experienced before. A peace that would take him away from the day's happenings, away from those awful sights and sounds and smells; a peace that he was hoping for. He felt his heart beating slower, his eyes slowly drooping, and soon, darkness.

Section Sixteen

Martin Becomes a Soldier

Sleep did not come easy for Martin that night. He tossed and turned and wondered about his leaving and telling his father of his plans. He got up out of bed, walked to the window and parted the curtains and looked out. He looked to the barn where the horses were kept and couldn't even fathom how many early mornings he had to go to the barn and feed the horses, brush them down, clean the area around the hay and then take one of the horses for a walk to get some needed exercise. He liked to go way out into the country and then test himself by running the horses, as fast as he could, and then returning to the barn secretly, as his father did not like for him to run them; too risky his father said. He would then have to rub them down and wipe them so that no sweat would show, just in case his father would come into the barn. But that was all in the past now. He quickly realized that he still had some packing to do if he was going to leave, but he grew tired and decided to lay down a bit.

Before he knew it, he woke up after a deep sleep, and remembered that he did not yet pack. As the sun was rising, he knew that if his plan were going to work, he would have to leave before his father got up in the morning. There would be no time for explanations now. He quickly and quietly got out of bed and got dressed. As he looked in the mirror, he thought of how he would look in the uniform of the Union army. He tried to stand up more straight now; his shoulders back and chest out, head back. All the things he had heard about.

With his bag packed, his hair slicked back and his cap on his head, he slowly went down the stairs and through the kitchen to the back door making sure he didn't make any noise. All was quiet and peaceful throughout the house. He couldn't take the mare from the barn and he didn't really want to walk back to town but that was the only choice he had. It was still early and as long as he got there before noon, he would be able to sign up as Sgt. Hull had told him to do.

As Martin walked down the dusty dirt road towards town, the sun rose higher in the sky, and he could feel the heat on his neck and the sweat dripping down his back. It was a warm day, not unusual for this time of year but he kept walking with his bag over his shoulder. The road to town was usually pretty empty, so he didn't think that he would see anyone he knew. After some time, he could see the town just ahead and his excitement made him forget about his sore feet from all the walking, his sweat stained shirt and his dusty pant legs.

Just then, a rider on horseback came up alongside him. "Hey boy, "he asked, "are you going into town?" It was Sgt. Hull. "Why sure, don't you remember me?" Sgt. Hull took off his hat, rubbed his chin a bit and said, "Why I'll be. You really are coming to sign up, aren't you? Well, climb up here and I will give you a lift into town. You look a might worn out from your walk." Martin swung his bag over his shoulder and climbed up behind Sgt. Hull and they rode quietly together into town.

Once they arrived in town, and they settled in at the post office where Martin had been the day before, Sgt. Hull said, "Here are your papers, son. You have to sign them to make it all legal. Once you do, you will be a soldier, a member of the Union army." Martin eagerly took the pen and papers, signed his name and then Sgt. Hull said: "Congratulations son. You are now a member of the Union army, instilled with all the rights of a soldier fighting for President Lincoln and the saving of the Union. You and the rest of the new recruits will be leaving here just after noon. There will be a train coming through town that will take us down to New York City. There you will receive your orders where to go, and you will meet your commanding officer. Men from all over the North are coming in to join."

Martin couldn't believe his ears. He was really a soldier. He was away from the foundry. He was away from...his father. He stopped for a minute and thought about that. What would his father think about his absence? He decided to write him as soon as he got to New York. After a while, he heard the train whistle down the tracks. He gathered his bag and ran down to the station landing. As he did so, he realized that he hadn't any breakfast and his stomach was beginning to grumble, that low, continuous noise that he often experienced on the way to the foundry when he had not had his breakfast. No time now though to get something to eat, and he certainly couldn't go to the general store, with his pack and papers. He would be recognized right away, so he told himself to just push on. This was, after all, a soldier's way of life. He didn't recognize any of the other recruits but he knew that this was his time. This was his time to make a difference.

The train pulled up and stopped with a slow screech of the wheels on the track. The dust filled the air and Martin turned away and covered his eyes to avoid getting dust in them. After he opened his eyes, he saw that the train was filled with young men, bound for battle, all looking out the windows. The others there began to load onto the train, finding seats among the cars. Martin did the same, and he found a seat next to another recruit and sat down, putting his pack in his lap and removing his cap and then ran his fingers through his hair. The train began to leave and suddenly there was a silence among the passengers. As Martin looked around, he saw the faces of the others. They were all young, maybe not as young as he, and yet, not really men. They had a nervous look about them all, there was not much conversation at first as they all knew that this was the first time each of them had ever put on the uniform of the Union army.

Martin opened his bag, pretending he knew what he was looking for, but really, just nervously passing time. He didn't know what to say to his fellow soldiers, not yet. He suddenly felt a tap on his shoulder and he turned to hear another soldier say, "Hey, my name is Oliver Malloy. You can call me Ollie." Martin replied, "My name is Martin, Martin Wickham. You can call me… (Martin thought for a second; he really hadn't been called anything except Martin in the past but wasn't really sure if now that he was a soldier he should adopt another name. He had heard of men dropping their given names for nicknames, but he really wasn't ready to do that, not yet) Martin."

"Well, pleased to meet you, Martin. Are you going to New York?" Ollie inquired." "I sure am," Martin replied. "Can't wait to get there. We should be there in a few hours. I bet our lives will never be the same, right?" he said a bit nervously. "You bet," responded Ollie. Then, they both got quiet, looked ahead and began to think about their journey as they sat back in their seats and stared out the window of the train.

As they moved, Martin wondered about Ollie. How old was he? Why did he join up? Where was he from? He had a ton of questions to be answered, but that would be for later. Now it was time to think and plan. Even though he was only sixteen, Martin had a sense of himself uncommon for other boys his age. Boys, he thought. That was funny. Here he was going off to war. Was he still a boy, or was he what he wanted to be, a man?

As he pondered his future, the time passed quickly. He could see the landscape outside the train changing. No longer were there fields and small towns. He began to see larger communities, more buildings, and more massive structures, unlike where he had spent his whole life. He had seen pictures of New York City in the papers that came to town, with its tall buildings, busy streets, and masses of people. As the train continued on, it was as if he was experiencing what he had seen in those pictures. Men and women, boys and girls, all dressed differently than he had ever seen before he left. He was entering the big city, New York City, and headed for his destiny.

Section Seventeen

Abigail Learns About Gettysburg

Being a man of many interests, some of them being geography and history, Mr. Handy made a point of talking with Abigail about both. "Now Abigail, since we have to go to Gettysburg, you might as well get acquainted with its history, as it is a rather remarkable place." Abigail sat on the stool in the living room, knowing that she had no choice. Her father wanted her to be educated well beyond what she learned in her everyday schooling. He often would sit with her in the evenings and talk with her about his own schooling; what he had learned from his teachers and from life itself.

"Abigail, Gettysburg has a long and established history. Mr. Lincoln has asked me to go there and get some more information about its agricultural contributions for the Union cause." "But father, I really am not interested in that. Mother told me that we would be having a vacation, not a history lesson!" John Handy thought a minute before he responded. He knew that

97

Abigail was a good student; he didn't want to come on too strong and make her disinterested.

"Abigail, did you know that Gettysburg was named for a Mr. Samuel Gettys, who moved there way back in 1761?" Not wanting to displease her father, Abigail said, "Of course not father, but could you tell me more?" "Sure can," Mr. Handy said as he sat up and with a twinkle in his eye. He added:" Now, something that few people know is this. When I was speaking with Mr. Lincoln about traveling down to Gettysburg, he told me a very unusual fact. It seems that Mr. Gettys married a woman named Mary Todd and that she was actually related to Mrs. Lincoln."

Mr. Handy then went on with what Abigail thought was a rather droll history of Gettysburg, but he moved ahead and told Abigail that Gettysburg, although not as big as Washington, was less than 100 miles away, had over 2500 citizens, and had a fairly large number of industries, including carriage manufacturing, shoemakers, and tanneries, along with the usual types of businesses found in many towns. "The farms around town were kept really neat, they had large and well-kept barns, many green fields and a great many, healthy livestock," he added. "There were also several educational institutions. And, most of all, the people who lived there were real friendly."

Abigail was not particularly impressed; Pittsburgh had been a much larger city with more to offer, and Washington had even more. Mr. Handy noticed that Abigail was not jumping up and down with joy at his latest attempt to get her interested. He tried to emphasize the richness of the Gettysburg area. He knew how Abigail loved horses and said, "Gettysburg also had a rich riding background. It had many fields where horses roamed freely, feeding off the landscape, and its many farms and grasslands were ideal for people like us who wanted to get away from the hustle and bustle of Washington."

What Mr. Handy did not say was that there were actually ten roads leading into the town of Gettysburg, from all different directions, which could be advantageous to both the North and South. In their meetings, Mr. Lincoln had told Mr. Handy that the Southern forces, led by General Robert E. Lee, had achieved many victories of late, and was ready to invade the North. Gettysburg could be an ideal target, with a dead-on course to Washington should he prevail in battle. If he secured a victory there, it could mean disaster to the North and cause many northerners to become disenchanted about war and to push for a settlement and peace with the South.

As he thought about this, Mr. Handy reminded himself that Abigail would have no understanding of or concern for this detail, and besides, he didn't want to worry her; she would only want to know what she would do once they got there.

"Abigail, we should probably start getting ready to go. I think we will be taking the train to Gettysburg. That will get us there much quicker than the horse and wagon," said Mr. Handy.

"Father, would it be alright to bring Rachel along with us?" questioned Abigail. "I am afraid not," Mr. Handy replied. "We might be gone for a while, and I am sure her folks would want her around their own home. Now, you get on and let your mother know that we will probably leave in a few days. The heat and work load here in Washington is beginning to bother me and I know that it will be more comfortable in Gettysburg."

Gary L. Kaplan

Mr. Handy continued:" I think I know some people in Gettysburg who we can meet up with who will be able to show us around. You know, kind of take us under their wing and treat us well. I hear that there are also a number of young ladies around your age who live there. You see, I have done my homework!" With this, Abigail brightened up, and thought to herself: this trip might not be so bad after all. She thanked her father for the information, and went straight away to her mother who was busying herself in the kitchen, getting ready for the dinner meal.

"Mother, I didn't say anything to father, but I was speaking with Robert earlier and I asked him about his earlier time, before he came to work with us. He didn't want to answer me. When I talked to him, he kind of choked up. He seemed to be holding something back from me." Mrs. Handy knew, of course, how Robert had come to work with them. She also knew that Abigail was too young to know of the horrors of slavery. She had lived in slave free areas all her life, and although she had read about it, and had seen men and women who had been slaves, she really didn't know of the conditions that existed day to day in the South, and most importantly, what Robert had been through in his earlier days, living through the conditions on the plantation. Further conversations about Robert would just have to wait.

From time to time, Mrs. Handy would sit with Robert while Mr. Handy was away at the White House or at some meeting, and talk about his past. Robert trusted Mrs. Handy and felt free to speak to her about his own history, so different from hers. He had told her about his woman, his child, his sale and eventual escape from the plantation in South Carolina and his eventual meeting

100

up with Mr. Handy in Pittsburgh, after traveling North along the Underground Railroad.

"Mrs. Handy," Robert would say. "Both you and Mr. Handy have treated me with so much kindness and respect. I don't know what I would have done if Mr. Handy had not taken me in that cold and rainy night in Pittsburgh. But he did, and I can't tell you how pleased I am of that. I know we are planning on going to Gettysburg for a spell, and I am mighty pleased to be asked to go along with you all."

Mrs. Handy knew that sometime soon, she would have to tell Abigail about Robert's past, but not without Robert's permission. Not now, she would not betray his trust, and she said to Abigail, "Abigail, we will just have to let Robert take his time with any explanations. For now, we have to pack for our trip."

Section Eighteen

Sarah and Tilly Are Off to Gettysburg

"It won't be easy to decide what to pack for the trip, especially one where we don't know how long we would be gone," Sarah said out loud. Sarah looked around her room and although she didn't have a whole lot of personal belongings, she still had her favorites, things she would want to take with her. She had her special boots that her father had given to her for her birthday, the ones that laced up the side of her leg and made her feel so grown up. She had her special hat, actually a baby blue, embroidered bonnet, that she saved for special occasions and kept in a round hat box that she had gotten in town after her mother said to her to pick one out as a reward for doing such good work on the farm. Of course, there was her favorite doll, Melinda, who she had to bring with her. Melinda was her constant companion when she was in her room. Dressed in a long flowing dress, similar to the color of Sarah's hat, and with nice shiny shoes, and a great big smile on her face, Melinda was Sarah's safeguard against loneliness.

Tilly, on the other hand had a real problem. This had been her home for years, and she had accumulated many personal items that she really didn't want to part with. She knew though that she could only take those items that she could carry, or ship. The house furnishings would have to stay. She and Sarah would be getting a ride to Charlottesville from their neighbor who had some business there, and from there they could take the train to Gettysburg. It would not be easy though; she had heard of soldiers commandeering the train for their own use and not really caring about other passengers. She hoped that she and Sarah would be treated fairly and with compassion, considering their circumstances.

"Sarah, it is time to go. Mr. Mitchell is waiting for us," Tilly shouted over the noise of the horses neighing and the roosters crowing. "Come and get in the wagon. All your things are already here." Sarah looked around at the front of the house, thinking about her move. Tilly did not want to look back; she felt that this might be the last time she would see the farm and didn't want to get too sentimental about it all. "Momma, what about the animals?" Sarah questioned. "Oh, don't worry dear. Mr. Mitchell said he would take good care of them while we were gone. He is a very kind man, and his wife really likes the animals so they will be in good hands. Now come."

Fortunately, Tilly had saved some money which would be just enough for the train fare to Gettysburg. She knew that troops were here and about, and she had heard that they were going to be moving to join the Army of Northern Virginia some time soon.

She just hoped she and Sarah could make it to Gettysburg without any incident, although she had not heard of any previous problems from the troops.

After several hours of traveling in the wagon, hitting just about every bump available in the dirt road, they finally got to Charlottesville. Sarah couldn't believe her eyes. She had never been to a city this big before and she stared at the numbers of people going to and fro with amazement. "Momma, where are all those people going?" Sarah asked with the kind of innocence only a child could muster up. Tilly tried to explain how some of the people worked for a living, some were shopping and probably some were, well, trying to figure out what to do tomorrow, just like they were. Some were dressed properly, as Tilly used to describe people she saw in town, away from the farms and plantations. Some indeed were in farm clothes, with the men wearing overalls, shoes and a shirt and the women wearing overalls as well, their long tresses of hair tied up in buns.

As they approached the train station, Mr. Mitchell pulled his wagon up to the sidewalk and quieted his horses. They both thanked Mr. Mitchell for his kindness and Tilly offered to pay him but he refused. "I can't take any money from you Tilly," Mr. Mitchell said. "And besides, you are going to need all you have to get you to Gettysburg," he added. "Now you both be careful. Mrs. Mitchell and I will look after your farm while you are away and we will expect to see you back soon." He thought to himself that this also might be the last time he might be seeing them, given the way the war was going. Who knew what tomorrow was going to bring. Sarah waved to Mr. Mitchell and grabbed her bag, as did Tilly, as they approached the train station to purchase their tickets for their journey North.

"Well honey, we are on our way," Tilly shouted to Sarah over the noise of the train engine as they boarded the passenger car. "Isn't this exciting?" she added. Sarah looked around and saw all kinds of people; men, women, little children, and soldiers getting ready to join some brigade for the first time, all nervous looking and remarkably young, all carrying bags, suitcases, really anything they could find to hold their belongings.

Sarah asked her mother, "Momma, how long will it take us to get to Gettysburg?"

Tilly replied, "I am not real sure honey. This train will make many stops along the way, so there is no telling for sure how long. But I brought some fixins for us to eat and I was told that the train has plenty of water, so we should have enough to provide for us." Now just sit back and try to relax. You can look out the window as we go and see all the pretty countryside."

Sarah listened to her mother and leaned back against the seat, making sure that Melinda was with her. She was both excited about the journey but also a little worried about leaving and going to a new place, so far away. What would she find there? Would she really find new friends?

As the train left the station and began to pick up speed, the click- clack of the iron wheels on the iron track began to hum a steady rhythm, so much so that when combined with the breezes blowing through the halfopened windows, Sarah became real tired and her eyes began to droop. She sat deeper in her seat, held onto Melinda and began thinking about going to Gettysburg and what she would do there. Her eyes got even heavier and as Tilly watched, Sarah slowly fell asleep. Melinda dropped from her hands but Tilly picked her up right away and placed her gently back in Sarah's lap. She knew this would be a long journey and where it would take them eventually, she could not tell. She knew that her cousin was expecting her but she had not seen her in years and hoped that the family connection was still strong. With that, she too leaned back in her seat and tried to relax and follow her own advice of taking in the scenery, looking out the window at the countryside as they left the town of Charlottesville.

Section Nineteen

Joshua Joins the Army

"Hey, you, boy, wake up!" shouted one tall, blonde haired, broad shouldered soldier as he kicked at Joshua with his right foot. He held his rifle with his left hand as the others stood around him, waiting for Joshua to make a move. "HEY," he repeated, this time shouting a little louder, as Joshua was awakened from what must have been a deep sleep. "What in blazes are you doing here," he shouted and waved his hat at Joshua with his right hand as if he were swatting a fly.

Joshua sat up and leaned harder against the tree and after he rubbed his eyes he looked up, not just at the man who yelled at him but at a group of men, all dressed in grey uniforms, some matched with the same type of pants and others with grey overcoats, or shirts with frayed collars and torn sleeves. Some had on hats, some not, but they all were carrying rifles and looked tired, dirty and in Joshua's eyes, mean. They were all standing around in a semi-circle in front of Joshua, with rifles in their hands. They were not pointed at Joshua, no reason to be, but just the same, they held them at the ready. He was a mere boy, and not expected to be seen in the woods. Especially since he was a black boy.

"What's your name, boy," another man said to Joshua. Joshua looked around and realized he was surrounded. He didn't know what to expect from these men. He had never seen men in uniform before, no matter what the color was. He had heard about the Confederate soldiers but had never seen one before. "My name is Joshua," he said. "Where are you from?" asked the first soldier. "What are you doing in these woods all by yourself?" asked another soldier, who was standing just next to Joshua. Joshua could feel the sweat drip off of his forehead and under his armpits as he thought of the best way to respond to these soldiers.

His mother had always told him that being honest was the best policy so he decided to take a chance and tell them the truth. "I used to live on a plantation not far from here, but the overseer beat my momma and she died. I was planning to get my revenge against him and went to his cabin and when I did, he tried to beat me too, but he tripped and fell against a table. He hit his head and then hit the ground and I saw blood and just ran. I kept running until I couldn't run no more and then leaned up against this here tree and I guess I fell asleep." "You guess you fell asleep?" shouted one of the soldiers. "Well I guess we found ourselves a little black boy who ran away from his master. I reckon we could get ourselves a might good reward for returning him, don't you think boys?" the first soldier said as he looked around him and at the others.

"Now you just wait a minute there corporal," said another soldier who had just come up to them on his horse. He was dressed a little different; he was older, with a grey beard and a long, plumed hat, a gold sash around his waist and a sword in a scabbard on the side of his horse. His horse was a big, black stallion with nostrils flaring as if he had been running for quite some time and had just settled down. His uniform was much cleaner than the uniforms of the other soldiers and he seemed to be in charge.

"What is going on here?" he said as he looked around at the other soldiers and then at Joshua. Joshua just sat still and watched, fearing that he might be brought back to the plantation where he surely would be whipped to no end.

The soldier who seemed to be in charge climbed down from his horse and walked up to Joshua. "Boy, my name is Lieutenant Johnson. These boys here are in my company and we are headed North. They don't mean you any harm; they are just soldiers who have been away from their homes for too long and don't know their manners." With that, the Lieutenant looked at the soldiers. There must have been 15 or 20 all together, not all of whom were standing around Joshua.

Lieutenant Johnson had joined the Confederacy while a student at West Point, that grand military academy up North. Joshua did not know this, but many of the Confederate officers had also gone to West Point. They were from the South, and when war broke out, rather than stay with the military in the North, many returned to the South and enlisted in the Confederate army as they felt it was their duty. Joshua would later learn that indeed, even General Robert E. Lee, the highest ranked soldier in the Confederate army, had gone to West Point. At the start of the war, Mr. Lincoln had asked him to stay with the North, but being from Virginia, General Lee thought it was his duty to stay on the side of the South and thereafter became the commander of the Army of Northern Virginia.

Joshua was grateful that Lieutenant Johnson was here; he was no longer afraid of what might happen next as Lieutenant Johnson seemed to have a calm around him and certainly was in command of the other soldiers. Joshua just didn't know now what was going to happen next. He still didn't like the way the other soldiers were looking at him. He had heard stories of how some escaped slaves had been found by Confederate soldiers and many were never heard from again. Would that be his fate as well?

Lieutenant Johnson thought a minute more and then spoke to Joshua: "I'll tell you what Joshua. I know things must have been hard for you on the plantation. What kind of work did you do?" Joshua thought a bit and responded: "Why, I did just about anything that needed to be done. I worked in the field a bit, took care of the animals, fixed things, and worked in my master's kitchen with my momma." As he said this, he thought again about his momma, how she looked that last day he saw her, but also about all the good times they spent together before that and his mind started to wander.

"Can you cook?" asked the first soldier, the corporal, who had woken him up and Joshua shook his head up and down and said, "Sure can!" "Well then, Lieutenant, I think we have found ourselves a new cook," he said in a sarcastic manner. As he said this, he looked over at Joshua in a not very friendly manner and he added: "We can use this boy. I bet he can cook up some mighty fine greens and ham hocks. I have a hankering for some of that, along with some coffee."

At this time, the Confederate army was not very lucky in terms of getting real coffee. As the war was progressing, the Union armies had formed a blockade around some of the southern states that kept most of the real coffee out of the territory occupied by the southern troops. Some coffee was smuggled in, some was traded for but most of all it was missed by the soldiers. There were even times when some soldiers, not having real coffee, would cook up substitutes. They would use roasted corn or rye, or chopped up greens and beets, grinding them up and then putting them in water and brewing them up until warm and colored. There was no caffeine in the brew, but the soldiers didn't care. They still liked it. It was better than nothing.

Lieutenant Johnson then remarked," Well, I guess the decision is made. Joshua, you can come with us and be our cook. Don't think we won't be watching you though, 'cause we will. If you make any attempt to leave, well I can't say that I will be able to control these here men if they get angry." Joshua thought again for a might, considered his options, and then said, "I would be most happy to be your cook, Lieutenant." All the men seemed pleased with this decision. All except the Corporal, who looked at Joshua with eyes that said, "I will be watching you boy." With that, they all got up and gathered their belongings. Now, Joshua had nothing but the clothes he was wearing and Lieutenant Johnson noticed that. "Here Joshua, you can put this pack on your shoulder. It has some extra clothes and even a pair of shoes which might fit you." Joshua thanked him, and threw the pack over his shoulder and began to walk with the group as they began to leave the area, still not sure about his new "adventure," but anxious to leave the area of the plantation.

Joshua thought it best to stay as close to Lieutenant Johnson as he could, not knowing what the feelings were of the other soldiers. He knew from talking to Mr. Washington back on the plantation that most of the southern soldiers had come from farms and plantations and didn't take too kindly to blacks being with them. Even though he was a boy, he was still black. And just because he wasn't on the plantation any more, he was still not free.

"Corporal Williams, we have to start moving," Lieutenant Johnson shouted over to Corporal Thomas Williams. "We have a long way to go if we are ever going to join up with the Confederate forces under General Longstreet. My orders were to get going as soon as possible. General Lee has this plan about going up to a town called Gettysburg, in Pennsylvania, and I don't want to miss that. Gettysburg is not far from Washington D.C. and if we can get that close, I am sure that we can beat this here Union army and take over the Capitol. That would certainly please President Davis as he sits in Richmond this very moment."

Now, Joshua didn't know anything about Gettysburg, or Richmond, or Jefferson Davis, the president of the Confederacy, but he did know about Washington D.C., the capital of the North and the town where President Abraham Lincoln lived. He had even heard about the President's move to free all the slaves by issuing the Emancipation Proclamation. That was the paper that the President signed not too long ago that gave the black people the right to be free. It was not taken too kindly by the South though, and he thought that Corporal Williams most likely didn't like it either. Nor did many of the other people in the South. He knew he had to try to stay clear of Corporal Williams. He reminded him of Mr. Potts, the way he talked to him and the way he looked at him. And he certainly didn't want any trouble. He would do his best to be a good cook and keep the men happy. That is, at least for the time being.

Section Twenty

Martin Gets His Assignment

Everywhere he looked, Martin saw other recruits. They were all different sizes, shapes, and ages, but they were all dressed in the same blue uniforms. It was like a vast sea of blue and he was feeling proud to be part of it. He had never seen such a large group of men together in one place before, let alone dressed like soldiers. "Hey, soldier, you there." When Martin didn't respond, the man tapped Martin on the shoulder and spoke up again: "Soldier, didn't you hear me?"

Martin turned around and looked up into the face of the tallest man he had ever seen. He was fully dressed in uniform and had a full beard the color of rust. Martin also saw the stripes on the man's sleeve and knew that he was an officer. "Sorry sir, I didn't know you were talking to me," Martin responded. "I am not real sure where I should go; maybe you can help me." There were crude tables set up around the room with soldiers sitting behind them and long lines of recruits waiting in front.

"Well, what's your name soldier?" "I am Lieutenant Benjamin Wilson, hooked up with the Third New York, Second

Division infantry based here in New York City, and just itching to head south to Washington. We have received our orders and are leaving this Friday. You had better go to one of those tables and check your orders. They have lists of all the new recruits and their assignments. If you are lucky enough, you will be part of my regiment. We have already seen action and I for one am ready to get back into the fray. I have even been to Washington and seen Mr. Lincoln. What a grand man he is too, willing to talk to us man to man and giving us hope for the reunification of this country. It's a real shame what the South has been doing, and now its time to set matters right. Where I come from, a man is a man, no matter what color he is, and its time we put a stop to this slavery issue and make this country whole again."

Martin listened intently to Lieutenant Wilson, and admired his determination, hoping that he could be assigned to his regiment. "Now, go boy, and get your papers. I will keep my hopes up that you are assigned to me. You look like a fine lad, well brought up and I am sure you will work yourself into becoming a true soldier for the Union." As Martin walked away, Lieutenant Wilson thought to himself how young Martin looked and wondered if he was really old enough to fight in battle. "I better keep an eye on that young man," he said to the man next to him. "Excuse me sir, while I go over and check on his papers."

As Martin was approaching one of the tables, Lieutenant Wilson stepped behind the table and whispered into the ear of one of the men sitting at the table. After just a few minutes, the man said to Martin: "Mr. Wickham, congratulations. You are now to be called Private Martin Wickham, assigned to the Third New York, Second Division Infantry and your commanding officer is Lieutenant Benjamin Wilson." Martin couldn't believe what he heard, and then saw the Lieutenant give him a wink and a nod as he pointed to a spot near the end of the hall, as if he wanted Martin to meet him there.

Martin gathered up his papers and moved away from the table, filled with hope about his new assignment. He recalled hearing his father say from time to time that things happen in life for a reason and one should not question the randomness or the surprise that accompanies something unexpected. He also had a good feeling about the Lieutenant, even though he couldn't really see his face behind that full beard. Martin wondered if he could ever grow a beard like that!

He hurried over to where he could see the Lieutenant standing a full head taller than the soldiers around him. He was careful not to drop his papers or his haversack, the canvas and leather bag that each soldier was given. It was a necessity to use the haversack to carry whatever couldn't be stuffed into pockets: food, eating utensils, diary, soap, well, just about anything. No larger than a small bag, it had a shoulder strap and a flap that covered the top. It was also lined so that the contents would not get wet if it rained, or if one had to go through water with it. Martin had heard about these haversacks, and also heard that the Confederates had some as well, although those were not as strong or as waterproof. Just another little advantage that the Union had over the South, Martin thought.

"Now men," Lieutenant Wilson began, "We are leaving Friday by train to head down to Washington. You new recruits will get used to the travel soon enough, but now its time to get all your things together. We will meet again in two hours across the street at the hotel and I will brief you on our plan, as well as on the rules I have set up for our regiment. We will be joining the more experienced men Friday and I expect you all to follow their lead. They are good, experienced men who have seen battle, have seen some of their friends and companions fall, and are ready to rejoin the fight. They might be a bit rough around the edges but you will not find another bunch of men as dedicated to the cause, and to each other, in this man's army.

As I have said to some of you already, we are all looking to end this war and rid the country of slavery. Back in Boston, where I hail from, there are black men and women who have been free for generations, have raised families, built up successful businesses and have become proud members of the community." This reminded Martin of the meetings that took place back at home, with both black and white members of his community, as they met at night and did their own planning. This also reminded him to write to his father too, since it had been days since he left the foundry and his home and he was sure that his father must be looking for him by now.

He found some paper and pen, and an envelope that was pre-printed with some symbols of the Union and after finding a quiet, secluded spot to write, he composed his letter:

Dear Father:

By now I am sure you are wondering where I went and what I was doing. I am fine. I have joined the Union army and will be heading to Washington with an infantry brigade soon. I don't want you to worry, or be mad. I had the good fortune to be assigned to the unit of a good man, the kind of man you would like. He is also against slavery, and hopes that the war will end soon. I feel a need to do what I can for our country, to keep it as free and united as it should be. You have taught me well and I intend to use what you have taught me and what the good Lord has given me to accomplish our goal. I do not know when I will have another chance to write to you.

I carry a picture of you as well as one of my dear mother who is always in my thoughts. I will learn a lot from my Lieutenant, and will use that learning to keep myself safe and valuable to our unit. We have many experienced men with us, and they are all of the same temperament about the war. I am looking forward to our journey and I want you to know how much I appreciate the guidance you have given me, and the struggles you have gone through while I have been growing up. I know it hasn't been an easy task.

I have every intention to return once the war is over. However, should the good Lord deem it necessary for me to surrender my life, then I will do so proudly and without remorse, for our cause is just. Keep me in your prayers, as you will be in mine. He then signed it: your loving son, Martin.

Martin asked those around him and found the place to post his letter. He felt at peace with himself and began to feel like he was a long way from his bedroom and those nights staring at the stars and wondering about his future. Looking around the room, he was wondering what was on the minds of the other soldiers as well.

Suddenly, he saw a familiar face and called out: "Ollie, hey Ollie, it's me, Martin, Martin Wickham." Ollie looked his way, smiled, and came over, and said, "Martin, what a surprise. I didn't think I would see you again and now here you are. Hey, what regiment have you been assigned to? I am with a Lieutenant

Wilson." Martin developed a grin on his face from ear to ear and responded, "Me too!" And with that, the two "men" took off to get a bite to eat and renew their friendship, one that would find them next to each other on a more fateful day.

As Friday dawned, Martin, Ollie and the rest of Lieutenant Wilson's regiment boarded the train bound for Washington. Each soldier had his own idea of what was going to happen once they got there and Martin was eager to see a different part of the country, one he had heard so much about and which was so different from his own. He also wondered about the war and what his role was to be.

Section Twenty-One

The Handys Arrive in Gettysburg

"M y, what a delightful station this is, don't you think, Abigail?" Mrs. Handy remarked to Abigail as the train pulled into the railroad station at Gettysburg, Pennsylvania. She was trying to make Abigail feel better after that long train ride from Washington. The train had left Washington and traveled to Baltimore, Maryland, where the cars were transferred to the Northern Central Railroad. From there, the train traveled to Hanover Junction, Pennsylvania and once again, the cars were transferred onto the branch line leading to Hanover and then Gettysburg.

"Abigail, we were lucky to have been able to take these trains," Mrs. Handy said, noting Abigail's seeming annoyance as she got down from the train onto the platform. "The railroad connection from Hanover to Gettysburg was just finished five years ago and this beautiful station itself only opened four years ago." Abigail was not impressed; she was not used to taking train rides at all, let alone a ride (or rides) that took almost eight hours from Washington. The train was comfortable enough for they had gotten seats with cushions and windows, so Abigail could see where she was going. She was no stranger to travel, having gone from Pittsburgh to Washington, and as the train passed through the country side, she could see the green grasses, and all sorts of trees that she didn't see in Washington, or even in Pittsburgh. She also saw fields of green, and horses and cattle, gently grazing.

"Just look around, Abigail. Look at how quaint this town is compared to old Pittsburgh and the confusion surrounding Washington," Mr. Handy commented. Once again, Abigail just rolled her eyes, thinking how she would much rather be back in Washington with Rachel, taking care of their animals, which now have been left in Rachel's safekeeping while she was to be away. "Father, how long will we have to be here, "Abigail inquired. "Now little lady, you had better hush yourself and have some appreciation for your folks bringing you down to this place," interjected Robert, who was carrying some of the suitcases down from the train. "Just smell the clean air and look around. This place is a might different from where we came from but it will be just fine for a spell."

Robert wondered to himself as well about how long they were going to be here. He had noticed the number of suitcases and bags the family had brought and it seemed like quite a bit of luggage for a short stay. He knew better to ask any further questions, not yet, and would wait till things settled a bit.

Rushing up to the station in a wagon led by two large horses was a rather portly man, middle-aged, who was nicely dressed and wearing a derby hat. He shouted, "Mr. Handy, is that you?"

He stopped and eased himself down from the seat of the wagon, walked over to Mr. Handy and introduced himself. "I am Hiram Sweeney, the Mayor of Gettysburg. Mr. Lincoln's secretary had wired us that you were coming for a spell and needed a residence suitable for your family and yourself. I have just the place; it has three bedrooms and a great field behind with horses and is just outside of town. If you would kindly get into my wagon, I can take you out there right now." Mr. Sweeney looked down at Abigail and said, "and little lady, you will be glad to know that just beyond the pasture, there is a family living there and they just happen to have a little girl. She looks to be just about your age as well. I am sure you both will get along right kindly."

Abigail knew by now that when adults were so optimistic about meeting someone new, oftentimes the opposite was true. The girl was probably uncouth, ill-mannered and hard to get along with. She probably didn't like animals either, Abigail thought to herself and she scrunched up her nose. Robert noticed that and knew that expression. He cautioned Abigail, "Missy, I told you to hold back now. Now you get along and help with this here baggage." Abigail obliged and picked up the smallest bag and lifted it into the wagon. "It's only a short ride from here folks," remarked Mr. Sweeney. "Just through the town and over that hill yonder and past the pond on the left. From the house, you could hear the crickets at night and if you listen real close, you can even hear the fish jumping in the pond." Abigail wondered if there were any stray dogs around!

As they rode through town, they all noticed the lack of young men. "Father, where is everybody?" Abigail asked her father. "Ever since the war started," Mr. Handy replied, "many of the younger men had left to join the Union army, taking that same train we took, but going in the opposite direction back to Washington. I expect that they will still be gone for a spell as this war seems to be carrying on a bit longer than any of us thought.

Mr. Handy recalled when the first shots were fired at Ft. Sumter in South Carolina, back in 1861, just shortly after Mr. Lincoln was elected President. President Lincoln thereafter had called up 75,000 troops for his army, and had them sign up for ninety days. Most folks thought that this little "affair" would not last long. However, not until the First Battle of Bull Run took place, and the Union troops, and the many well wishers who were watching the battle on the nearby hills, with their picnic baskets and blankets and fine clothes fled in horror as the Confederate troops put on a show of arms and desire did the threat of a longer war really take hold. That defeat meant that this was no longer going to be a mere skirmish.

Mr. Handy knew that southern troops were on the march North. The president had advised him of this before he left Washington. He also knew that there were plenty of Northern troops in the vicinity and felt that Gettysburg was still a safe place to be. It was almost mid-year, and as summer was rapidly approaching, battles were still going on a long way away. Still, he was hoping that this trip would be shorter, rather than longer. He didn't want his family to have to worry about the war, or witness any of the atrocities associated with the war, atrocities he had secretly been reading about that occurred on both sides.

As they finally approached the house, Mr. Sweeney said, "Well folks, here we are. Just get down from the wagon and have a look see. We knew you were coming and that you would probably be hungry and thirsty so my wife had some food prepared. And for you Abigail, we have a big pitcher of fresh lemonade."

They all got down and Robert began to carry the bags into the house, an old, rather large farmhouse that had several steps leading up to a wide porch from where you could sit and look out over the fields and see the pond. "The family that lived here had to leave, Mr. Handy, "Mr. Sweeney remarked, "it was rather sudden and they most likely will not be coming back anytime soon." Mr. Sweeney pulled Mr. Handy aside and whispered, "You see, they lost two boys at the battle of Bull Run, the second one, and just couldn't stay on anymore. Too hard to think about it, so they went back up to New York to stay with family. They gave us the ok to use their house as we saw fit."

"I will have to let Mr. Lincoln know of their generosity, and of their loss, Mr. Sweeney," Mr. Handy stated, and then made a note to do so. As he looked out from the porch, he saw Abigail walking with her glass of lemonade around the side of the house. Just then he heard a shout, "Father, come look!" It was Abigail's voice and as he ran around the side of the house he saw a familiar sight, one that brought a smile to his face.

"Molly, come here," he shouted to his wife, who was already coming around the side of the house as well. They both looked and saw that Abigail had discovered a dog with three little pups under the porch around back, settled into a little pen. She was cuddling the pups as the mother dog was licking her cheek and resting in her lap. "These pups can't be any more than a couple of weeks old," Abigail shouted excitedly. "They must have belonged to the family that left. Can we keep them?" Abigail asked excitedly.

"Well of course you can, Abigail," as both Mr. and Mrs. Handy responded simultaneously, and then they both looked at each other and laughed together. "It seems we now have a new branch of the Abigail Handy dog rescue service," Mrs. Handy spoke out loud. They both laughed again and hoped that this discovery would ease their time at Gettysburg, as they watched Abigail treat those pups and the momma as her own.

"Mr. Handy," Mr. Sweeney offered, "You can use the upper floor for your office needs. We have brought a nice desk and table and chairs for you, which will allow you to work away from the family downstairs. Anytime you want to send a telegram back to Washington, you let me know and I will have it taken care of. We also have a well-stocked general store in town. I see that you have brought your boy with you..." Mr. Handy interrupted Mr. Sweeney and said, "Robert is more than our help Mr. Sweeney. He is a free man and is really part of our family and should be treated as so, if that is all right with you. He has been with us for many years, has been a constant contributor to our household and a source of inspiration to us for all that he has gone through. He is to be treated with the utmost respect." "My apologies, sir," Mr. Sweeney responded. I will see to it that he is treated well."

"I had better be going now," Mr. Sweeney announced to them all. "It's time for me to get back home. You will see that there is a wagon and two good horses in the barn behind the house. You know the way into town, so if you need me, just ask anyone and they will know how to find me." With that, Mr. Sweeney got back up on his wagon and left, and as he passed Abigail, he called out: "So long Abigail. You take care and maybe tomorrow you can meet your neighbors. And take care of them pups." "Thank you, Mr. Sweeney," Abigail waved and replied. "I will, and see you soon."

In the kitchen, Mrs. Handy said, "Oh, John, do you really think it is safe here for us? You know what they were saying in Washington about the rebels." "Don't worry dear," he said. "Mr. Lincoln assured me that we wouldn't be here for a great length of time. He wanted me and us to take a break from the turmoil in Washington as well as from the spring heat and humidity. He knew how that affected you so, compared to the climate in Pittsburgh. And, if need be, it is only a day's ride by train back to Washington. So, if you feel the need, you and Abigail can leave and visit and then come back. Mrs. Lincoln would have loved to come to visit us here, but she is tied up in Washington, but does give you her regards." With that, they both looked out the window and saw Abigail playing with the dogs, and Robert looked at them all, wondering what it would be like to be with a real family again, as he absentmindedly fingered the scar on his cheek which no longer hurt to the touch, but hurt in his heart as if he was receiving the blow that caused the scar this very day.

Section- Twenty-Two

Sarah Finds a Friend

"**M**other, I can't believe how beautiful this country is. Look out the window, look!" Sarah pushed at her mother's elbow and Tilly opened her eyes. She had been sleeping but now with a gentle poke in her rib from Sarah, her dreams of the farm and John were quickly pushed aside and replaced with the words from her daughter. "Mother, look at all those horses," Sarah cried out. "I have never seen so many at one time before and aren't they beautiful?"

Tilly straightened herself and replied, "Why, I don't think I have seen such wondrous creatures before, Sarah." As the train raced its way down the tracks, both Sarah and Tilly looked at the horses as they romped past them, headed for who knows where. "Are we almost there yet?" Sarah asked. Tilly replied: "The conductor told me that Gettysburg was just a short distance ahead dear. We had better get our things together. My cousin Sally will be meeting us at the train station."

As they got themselves together, and Sarah found Melinda among her packages, putting her in the crook of her arm, while

Tilly excitedly thought about her cousin and the times they had as children, long before the war and before she had met her husband and Sarah's father. She could recall long, summer evenings sitting with the family, enjoying each other's company, sipping on ice-cold lemonade as the younger children would play in front of the house. Games of hide and seek and tag were just some of the games they played. Oh, to be young again, she thought to herself. But times have changed, and reality now dictates a different time, different place, and different responsibilities.

"Sarah, I haven't told you yet, but my cousin has three children, two boys and a girl. And, the girl is just about your age, give or take a year or two. I can't remember right now whether she would be 13 or 14 by now. But I do know that she loves horses and their farm has several. Now, her husband has gone off to war, just like your daddy, so I am sure you girls will have plenty to talk about and do while we are visiting. You remember to be on your best manners though; this is not our house or farm and you will have to do your share of chores." "I know Mother," said Sarah, knowing full well that she could not just sit back and have others do things for her. She was used to hard work back on her own farm and actually liked the physical part of the farm work especially when she could work with the animals.

"Sarah, look." Tilly pointed out the window and Sarah could see the town beginning to show on the horizon. "We should be there in just a few minutes," Tilly added. Just then, the conductor came through the car, shouting, "Gettysburg, all off for Gettysburg." He continued on through the car, through the door and into the next car. "When we stop, Sarah, we have to make sure that we get all of our baggage. The train will not wait long and we don't want to forget anything."

As the train slowed and approached the station, Tilly looked out her window and could see a woman with a buckboard and horses waiting near the tracks. It had been years since they were last together, but she could not forget her cousin's face. She was by herself and when she saw Tilly, she began to wave with both hands, sitting up tall in the seat of the wagon.

The train finally came to a halt with a rush of steam and screeching of the brakes and, they got off the train while the baggage handlers unloaded the baggage for all the passengers. "Sarah, please count those bags. I want to head over to see Sally and I don't want to lose anything." With that, Tilly ran to meet Sally who got down from her perch on the buckboard, ran towards Tilly and both women hugged as if they were schoolgirls again. Neither spoke; it had been so long since they had seen each other and now it was time just to be with each other for a spell. "I counted 7 bags Mother," Sarah yelled, "and I even have Melinda, holding her up in the air so Tilly could see." Sarah hurried over to her mother and Sally.

"Sarah, I want you to meet my cousin, Sally. Sally, this is my daughter, Sarah," said Tilly with a pride only a mother could show. "How do you do Sally," said Sarah. "Oh, you don't have to be so formal with me Sarah," Sally responded. "We are all family. Now get yourself up here and I will have one of the baggage handlers pick up your things. You say you had seven bags?" "Yes, Ma'am," said Sarah somewhat sheepishly, as she didn't know what kind of person Sally was or really how understanding she was about them joining them on the farm.

"I told my kids that we would be back in time for dinner so we had better hurry," Sally announced. "Our ride is not too long, but we will have to stop in town to pick up a few provisions that I ordered on the way out here. It won't take but a few minutes."

After stopping at the general store and picking up several bags of groceries, they continued on into the countryside, passing some ponds and large trees, unknown to Sarah, and finally arrived at the ranch. Sarah couldn't believe how nice it looked compared to her farm back in South Carolina. The grass was green and the crops were springing up from the ground. Late spring in Gettysburg sure is pretty, Sarah thought to herself.

"Mother, mother, you're back," shouted a voice from the house. Out came a young girl, no more than thirteen or fourteen, and as she ran down the steps, Sarah could see how much she looked like her mother: She had long brown hair tied in a bow behind her head, a blue colored flowing skirt, tight fitting blouse of cotton and a pair of dark brown riding boots, obviously used often as they were caked with mud and worn around the front of the toes.

"Kathy," announced Sally, this is my cousin, Tilly, and her daughter, Sarah." "Well hello, and pleased to meet you," replied Kathy. They all hugged again, and Sally remarked that the boys must be out in the pasture. "They will be back soon, so let's go into the house. They can pick up the bags and bring them when they get back," Sally said.

"Tilly, I am so glad you wrote to me. I was wondering what had happened to you over the years. You sure look fine but I am sure you must be tired after that long trip," Sally offered. "I would like to sit for a spell Sally," Tilly replied. "Girls, why don't you both go on upstairs," Sally directed. "Kathy, show Sarah where she can put her things. I hope you girls don't mind sharing a room. I doubt if you will want to stay with the boys," Sally joked. Both Kathy and Sarah looked at each other and laughed as they ran up the stairs and disappeared into one of the rooms.

"Now you sit, Tilly, and tell me all about this here farm of yours and your husband John," Sally said with more than just mild concern in her voice. "When did you hear from him last?" "It's been almost a year now Sally, and I haven't the heart to tell Sarah how worried I am that he may not be coming back. I have no idea where he is and every night when I go to bed I just lay there thinking of how it must be for him to be away from the farm, from us, and...."

"Now just you hold on there, woman," Sally commented. "You must have faith in the fact that he will return. Without faith and hope, you will drive yourself into a state of depression, or worse. You have a girl to bring up just as I have my children to take care of and being depressed will stop you from moving forward. I want you to stay here as long as you need to; I can actually use the company anyway and having Sarah be with Kathy will take some of the pressure off of her having to deal with the boys every day. They are good boys, but still, they can be annoying to a fourteen- year old girl!" With that, they both laughed and gave each other another hug.

"Help me put these groceries away would you dear?" Sally said as they walked into the kitchen. "Those young boys don't know how to stop eating so we had better start making dinner. We can talk about family later after the kids are asleep."

Tilly started to help unpack and as she did so, she experienced a sense of calmness and comfort that she hadn't had for some time. She felt she had made a good decision by coming here.

"You can have this bed Sarah," Kathy said as she motioned over to the side of the room. "The boys will be next door and they won't bother us once they go to sleep."

Sarah looked around the room and marveled at how nice Kathy's room looked. She had her own bed with velvety blankets and fluffy pillows the color of indigo. She had painted walls, the color of light colored grass and in one corner was a pine desk with a mirror hanging over it. She even had yellow print curtains on her window which looked out over the fields of soybeans and corn.

How different this farm was from her own farm that now lay in disuse and disarray, the farm she had just left a short time ago. Her thoughts also drifted to the face of her father, an almost everyday occurrence, and she wondered where he was. Was he alive? Was he safe? Would he be seeing the same kind of sights she was seeing? She didn't want to think about anything worse than that. Fortunately, Kathy saw the dreamy expression on Sarah's face and said," Let's go outside. I want to show you the barn and the animals." Sarah's mood changed and she became excited and they both ran down the stairs, past the kitchen and out into the yard area, holding hands just like two old friends.

"You know Tilly, since my husband Simon has been away, I have had to take on the role of mother and father to my kids. It has not been easy, especially with the boys and all. But at least I know where Simon is. He is able to send letters from time to time and lets me know what he is up to. He is not in the regular army. He had a fall last year while he was making hay and tore up his knee.

When enlistment came around and all the men signed up, he felt a need to join in but because of his knee, he couldn't join the infantry. He was able to talk to some people though and he got himself a desk job in Washington so we hear from him from time to time. Why, he even came out here a few months back to visit; he had some kind of leave or something, but then he went back. The kids are doing ok with it and all but I can only imagine how poor Sarah must be missing John. We will do our best to make life here for you both as best as it can be. Don't you worry." Tilly felt encouraged and was grateful for Sally's kindness, and her direct approach to Tilly's circumstances. She, too, thought of John, and as Sarah did earlier, thought about whether he was alive and safe.

Section Twenty-Three

Life In a Confederate Camp for Joshua

From what Joshua could determine, the regiment that he was now affiliated with lacked many of the essentials that a traveling army would need. The war had been going on for over two years now, and the southern soldiers no longer were dressed in their cadet gray, which was now in short demand due to the running out of supplies. The soldiers he was camping with often had their locally dyed, handmade outfits, sometimes in a brownish color that was often called butternut, sometimes just in overalls and shirt with suspenders and shoes that had seen better days.

Joshua would also overhear the soldiers complaining about the lack of proper food, and how the northern soldiers were so much better fed and supplied. Since the war had been dragging on, Confederate soldiers, when possible, received foodstuffs from home, but even then, they often were spoiled or arrived in broken parcels, when they could even be found. Hardtack and salt pork were supplied as best as could be done, and cooking was one way to salvage previously inconsumable food. Joshua knew how to add herbs and some spices to enhance the flavor of food, but in the camps, these were rarely available, so he had to make do with what he had. This did not help in his treatment by the other soldiers though; Corporal Williams continued to be a thorn in his side. "Boy, do you call this food?" Corporal Williams shouted to Joshua as he bit into the salt pork that Joshua tried to make more palatable by adding some herbs he found nearby the camp. "Boy, are you trying to make us all sick?" Corporal Williams continued. Since bad cooking was the cause of a lot of the intestinal problems that soldiers, both North and South, experienced, each camp cook tried to do his best to provide food that was at least edible, if not wholesome.

Corporal Williams walked over to Joshua and threw his plate down on the ground in front of him and yelled, " Ain't never tasted anything so bad before. I thought you said you could cook! I knew we shouldn't have taken you on; we should just have shot you then and there, you little runaway." Just then Lieutenant Johnson walked up and said, "Corporal, I think it's about time you and the others do a little drilling out beyond the camp. Let me have a talk with Joshua here." "But Lieutenant," Corporal Williams started to protest. "No Corporal, I have given you my order. We don't know how soon we will have to leave to head North, so the sooner you all learn how to organize yourselves and get along, the sooner we can be a successful, combative unit." With that, Corporal Williams and the rest took off, noticeably grumbling under their collective breaths.

Joshua issued a sigh of relief, but didn't like the look in the eyes of Corporal Williams as he turned to leave. There was anger there. No, more than anger. He had the eyes of hatred and revenge and Joshua knew that he had better stay on the good side of Lieutenant Johnson to stay safe. Still, he could feel his hands shake with nervousness as he tried to accept his new role as cook.

"Joshua, you have to understand one thing," offered Lieutenant Johnson. "These men have been away from home for a long time, without knowing what was happening to their families and properties back home. They can get irritable, especially Corporal Williams. He lost his farm and one of his brothers back home after the war started and seems bent on blaming the world generally, and the poor blacks specifically, for all his troubles. You best try to ignore his rants and ravings when you can, and I will see what I can do about it as well. Now I think you had better take a look and see what supplies we have for our dinner, as the boys will be mighty hungry when they get back."

Getting away from this group of soldiers was definitely an idea that Joshua mulled around his mind, as he prepped the food for dinner. He also knew that without knowing where to go or how far he was from any towns or villages, at least he had some protection with Lieutenant Johnson. For a young black boy to be traveling by himself during these times was not a very safe move, especially since he was camped with a certain Corporal.

He tried to take in his surroundings as best he could, and knew that the more he watched, listened and remembered, the faster he would gain an understanding of his whereabouts. His desire to escape and join the Underground Railroad was strong on his mind. He just hoped that his plan would not be thwarted by the actions of Corporal Williams. Still, he did not relish wearing the southern colors, although that was his only choice, at least for now. He was not used to the traveling either, but he knew that he had gone quite a way from the Andrews plantation and was probably forgotten by now.

He thought of his mother with a sadness that would come and go daily and hoped that Peter had taken care of matters after he left. He began to recall all the good times he and his mother had experienced over the years, and how she had taken care of him. As for Mr. Potts, well, that was another matter; Joshua thought that he had gotten what he deserved and promised himself that it was not his fault that Mr. Potts had met his untimely end. At the same time, he was free from plantation life.

"Gently boy, gently," announced Lieutenant Johnson as he walked up behind Joshua. "You don't have to pound that meat that hard!" Joshua's thoughts had drifted back to when he was on the plantation, taking orders from Mr. Potts, as he was trying to tenderize some of the meat that the soldiers recently brought to camp and in thinking about Mr. Potts, his anger and sadness came through his hands.

"Oh, I'm sorry sir," Joshua replied. He quickly put down the hammer like tool he used and continued," I didn't mean no harm, sir. I was just thinking about something else and..." "Never you mind Joshua," Lieutenant Johnson said. "You have been doing real good for us these past weeks and I appreciate what you have gone through both on the plantation and here. I just want you to know that not all southerners own slaves, or even believe in slavery."

"As a matter of fact, most of these boys fighting for the South were not slave owners at all, and have no real feeling either way. A lot of them were just tired of hearing about how the North was going to come down to their lands and take over, kick them off their farms, and make them live a new way of life. They were then and still are now defending their land and their way of life, and don't really mean any harm to you or to your fellow blacks.

My family back in Tennessee did not own slaves; we had a hardware store and sold general goods. After I enrolled at West Point, and the war broke out, I thought it best to fight with my family and friends, all of whom joined the Confederacy. You see, I am not in favor of war either and will be glad when it ends. I just hope that when it does, we have settled our differences. I don't like to see men die on either side and I certainly don't want my men to experience the losses that I have heard about. We all have families to go back to, and one of my goals is to see that it happens."

Joshua liked the Lieutenant; he was thoughtful, kind, and listened to Joshua, especially after he told the Lieutenant about his life on the plantation, and of his mother's death. He even told him what he knew about his father, hoping beyond hope that one day he would see him again. But for now, he was part of the Confederate army, like it or not.

Martin Experiences Real Military Life

"Hey Ollie, let's get something to eat. I am famished and since we don't have to report until 5:00, we can eat and maybe look around this town." Martin spoke confidently, knowing that he really was nervous about being in Washington, D.C. for the first time. He had heard about it from his father and from the newspapers he had read that had come to his father's house. On the train ride down from New York, he and Ollie got to know each other much better, and even though Ollie was three years older than Martin, they still got along well, trading stories of hunting, fishing and the like.

Everywhere he looked, Martin could see soldiers in very different styles of dress, either marching down the long, unpaved streets, or sitting on the sides of the street, waiting for their regiments to move out. Martin had not yet been told where they were to go; they heard stories about Richmond, and how capturing Richmond could make the war end much quicker. By now, he had also heard about battles won and lost by the Union, battles like Bull Run, Shiloh, Antietam and most recently, the Battle of Fredericksburg. War fever was rampant in Washington, and Martin was eager to join the fray, that is until he heard stories of the dead and wounded and the hardships suffered by soldiers on both sides. As he and Ollie walked around town, he was also able to see some of the soldiers who had already come back from battle, the tired, wounded, and bandaged. Sometimes, helpless soldiers were waiting for medical care, or just sitting somewhere to rest their weary bodies.

Martin could feel his stomach becoming nervous and tighten with anxiety as he looked upon the throngs of once proud and courageous souls, now relegated to the aftermaths of real war.

"Martin, what's bothering you?" asked Ollie as they stopped at one of the many gathering places of the soldiers. "Ollie, I was really looking forward to entering the fighting all the way down here from New York. It sounded so, so exciting. Now, after seeing all these wounded soldiers, I am not so sure." "Now you just wait a minute there, shorty," Ollie responded. "We didn't come all this way for you to get cold feet. You know how important our jobs are, especially now that we are here in Washington. Why, I hear that President Lincoln himself was going to talk to the new recruits tomorrow. You can't let your gut rule your brain, now, can you?"

Martin wasn't sure how to reply; he had mixed feelings but saw the expression on Ollie's face, one of encouragement, and decided that Ollie was right. They were here to do a job and surely with the numbers that the Union had, they would surely prevail. "Look there, Martin," Ollie said as he motioned over to the other side of the street. "Isn't that Mr.

Lincoln? Why it sure is. Martin, there is the President himself." Martin turned and saw President Lincoln as he was walking with some other well-dressed men and was deep in conversation. He stood out so, with his black top hat and long coat. He was at least a head taller than the rest of the men, and was in deep conversation. "I can't believe that is really him, Ollie," Martin offered. As President Lincoln walked down the sidewalk, all eyes turned to him and the people just stared. "Why, he is on the way to the Capitol," Martin stated. All of a sudden, Martin's nervousness and anxiety disappeared, replaced by a sense of pride. He was actually seeing the President of the United States, right before his very eyes.

"Martin, we had better be getting back. We don't want to be late for roll call." Ollie now pulled on his jacket and Martin turned and said, "Ollie, I was not feeling too well before. But now that I have seen the President I have a whole new way of feeling. I remember his speeches about keeping the Union together. Do you remember his House Divided speech?" "I can't say that I do," Ollie replied. "But you know by now that book learning and reading are not my best assets." Martin laughed and told Ollie how he had read in the newspapers about Mr. Lincoln's many speeches. Then, they both laughed and began walking back to their regiment, Martin forgetting about his fears.

As they entered the compound where the 3rd New York, Second Division infantry was gathering, Martin and Ollie could hear Lieutenant Wilson speaking to the group. "Men, we should be receiving orders tomorrow or the next day as to our destination.

Before we do, I want to make sure that you all have your gear in order. Once we leave, we will be going as one unit, and I want to make sure that you all present yourselves in a respectful manner." Lieutenant Wilson continued, discussing general plans of organization for the regiment, and the like. "Now, I don't mean to make anyone nervous, or scared, but in the realities of war, there is a good chance that not everyone will be coming back. We have a tremendous job to do, as you know, and it is our hope that we will prevail. As to what cost, only the almighty knows. But for now, we are one and we will go into battle, nor matter where, as one.

The group was silent, each man choosing not to look up for fear of making contact with someone else's eyes. Martin thought about the foundry, his father, and his room, and how he used to lie on his bed and look at the stars at night. He wondered to himself whether he would ever return to that idyllic setting, and his boring existence.

The next morning, bright and early, as Martin was gathering his clothes and stuffing his haversack with his personals, being sure not to dislodge his food knife and pocket watch that he brought with him. The Second Division was waiting for Lieutenant Wilson and his announcement. He walked in with a solemn, yet determined look on his face, followed by his fellow officers. "Men, we have received our orders. Day after tomorrow, we will be leaving. We have gotten word that General Lee and his Army of Northern Virginia are moving with the goal to enter Union territory. Based upon that, our orders are to move towards a town named Gettysburg, in Pennsylvania. It is a pleasant place, surrounded by generous fields and rolling hills and the feeling from here in Washington is that Lee will try to take Gettysburg and move onto Washington. There are several regiments who will be joining us and we will make a stand there and hopefully put an end to this war."

Martin and Ollie looked at each other with a confidence that neither one had before. Only sixteen years old, Martin was now going to embark upon an adventure he would never forget. Would he be ready to answer the call? Only time would tell!

Section Twenty-Five

Abigail Plans to Go to Town

"Mama, we have been here a whole week, and I haven't even been to town once. Why, I'll bet that there are all kinds of girls living in and around town, who are my age. I sure would like to see them. Can we take a ride into town, please!" Abigail liked her new surroundings, and loved taking care of the dogs on the property. Still, it wasn't her own house and they weren't her own dogs.

"Mother," Abigail now spoke up in a more serious tone, "Can we go today, please." Mrs. Handy thought for a moment, considered her alternatives, and realized that she, too, missed the contact with people in town. She had been spending a great deal of time at the house, making it comfortable, or as comfortable as it could be, for Mr. Handy. Still, she needed some new company, people other than her own family, and Mrs. Handy replied, "Sure, Abigail. I will make arrangements to have the wagon made ready for us. I need to do some shopping anyway, and we can spend the afternoon looking around. I have heard that there are a number of shops in town that cater to young ladies."

Abigail almost burst with enthusiasm when she heard this news. "Mama, I can be ready in a flash. Would you tell Daddy about our adventure?" "I sure will sweetie; just give me a little time to get ready myself, and then I will tell your father about our little plan. I am sure he won't mind."

As she approached her husband who was sitting in the living room, attending to some papers that he received from Washington, Mrs. Handy, a little hesitant in bringing up the subject, since she knew her husband was concerned for their safety, said, "John, it's been a full week, and it is about time that we make a trip into town.

Mr. Sweeny seems like an honest man, maybe a little one sided on his feelings about Robert, but he hasn't made any problem yet. Both Abigail and I would love to have some contact with people other than him and his family. Besides, as mayor of this Gettysburg, I am sure he wouldn't want any trouble from his guests from Washington!"

Mr. Handy could not argue with his wife. He knew that when she had her mind made up, well, there was not much he could do to alter her plan. "Mother," he replied, "I will tell Robert to get the wagon ready. I have some correspondence to get out today, but Robert can take you and Abigail into town straight away." He thought for a moment about how Mr. Sweeney first reacted to Robert's presence, but was sure that by now, there would be no problem. "Maybe you can stop into Mr. Sweeney's office in town and pay our respects. He really has been a help to us in getting settled here." Mrs. Handy thought for a moment and said, "John, I would like to spend the afternoon in town as well, to take in the sights, maybe meet some people, and see how they feel about this here war."

"Now, now. We must not push this war thing too far," Mr. Handy offered. "We don't know how people really feel and I wouldn't want to start anything that might make our stay less welcome, in case there are some people with Southern leanings, especially if you take Robert with you. He has been with us so long that we forget that he is different from us. We have treated him well, as one of our own, but we are not at home now. I don't want you to have any problem going into town accompanied by a black man. People in town might not be as open to that as we are."

"Why John," she said, "I can't believe you are saying that." She started to get flushed in the face, and John knew he overstepped his bounds. "Ok, I understand where you are coming from," John said. "I am just a little nervous, given all the communication I have been receiving lately from the telegraph office about the advancement of the Southern troops." Mrs. Handy turned in surprise. "What communications, John?"

Mr. Handy thought to himself that it might be better to open with the truth now, rather than later. "Mother, (he always started with a tone of seriousness and forthrightness when he was talking about an issue of importance) it looks like a number of troops from the Army of the Potomac are heading down to Gettysburg. We have heard that Lee and some of his generals are planning on a move towards Washington, and we are planning on heading him off. I don't think there will be a problem, but just in case, I have arranged for a plan to leave by wagon and then railroad, just in case some fighting starts." "Oh John, now you have me worried," Mrs. Handy said as she wrung the handkerchief in her hands. "What should we say to Abigail?" "Nothing now," Mr. Handy replied, not knowing how to make it any more comfortable. "She doesn't have to know anything except that you and her and Robert are going for an afternoon visit. Now, go get ready and you had better leave and get back before it gets dark." It was easy to see that Mr. Handy was ill at ease with his statements, and despite telling his wife that all was well, he didn't feel the same, based upon his mailings from Washington, and his conversations with Mr. Sweeney.

He knew that General Grant was trying to capture Vicksburg, Mississippi, as a way to form a stranglehold on the Confederacy and cut off access to the Mississippi River, and by all accounts, he was gaining the upper hand. Still, with this war going on for over two years, there was no telling what General Lee would be up to, especially after the Union army loss at Fredericksburg, Virginia. Still, his family's life had to go on, and despite his misgivings, he told himself that going into town would be a nice release for his family.

Section Twenty-Six

Sarah and Kathy Explore Gettysburg

I t wasn't until the next morning, after she woke up and the sun was shining into her window, that Sarah actually realized that she was no longer on the farm. Well, she knew, but the reality of what she was seeing was just beginning to sink in. Kathy was not in the room and Sarah got up and walked to the window. As she looked out at the fields and the pond that was just beyond the corn that was beginning to sprout out of the soil, she could see that Kathy was already out doing chores. Tugging at the reins of two horses, Kathy was bringing them to the area behind the house, walking them around the pond first, and then tying them up to the hitching post just behind the kitchen. What beautiful horses she thought to herself!

As she looked around the room again, she noticed some of the more obvious signs that this was indeed the room of a young girl, signs she missed the night before. Kathy's collection of rag dolls was sitting upright on her bed, up against the pillows and each dressed in frills and colored cloth, as if they were dressed and ready to attend a Sunday church function. "Sarah, can you come downstairs for breakfast?" Sarah's mother was at the foot of the stairs, already dressed and ready to start her and Sarah's new life in Gettysburg. "Sarah, did you hear me?" Tilly's voice was a little louder now. "Alright mother, I hear you," replied Sarah. "I will be right down."

Sarah pulled on her britches and boots and threw a cotton shirt over her head and as she smelled the bacon frying in the kitchen, she knew that this would be an exciting day. She ran down the stairs and entered the kitchen, and saw that not only Kathy and Sally and her mother were there, but two dark haired boys who looked so much alike that she could swear she was looking at a mirror reflection. The twin boys, Harry and Peter, were already munching down their breakfast. They were big for their age and each had a crop of dark hair that hung over their eyes. "Boys," stated Sally, "meet your cousin, Sarah." They looked up just long enough to make eye contact with Sarah, nodded, and then proceeded to continue eating like there was no tomorrow. "Boys, mind your manners," Sally spoke up with a louder, more resonant voice.

"That's ok Sally," remarked Tilly. "Let them eat. When they are through, they can help show Sarah around the ranch." Tilly looked over to Sarah, gave her a wink, and then placed a plate of bacon and eggs and some buttered bread on the table. "Sarah, here, sit and have some breakfast," Tilly said. "Kathy should be back in just a shake."

"I know mother; I saw her out the window with two horses," Sarah said. Sally looked over to Tilly once again and said," Oh, you mean the two horses that you girls are going to ride into town on? Sarah looked up with the brightest eyes one could imagine and said, "Are you serious? You mean I will actually be able to ride today?"

Sarah was so excited that she didn't even touch her breakfast and she had to be reminded that before they could go, she needed first to finish her breakfast, and complete the chores that Kathy had started. Then, they would be able to go.

"Harry, Peter, after you finish and do your dishes, will you show Sarah around the barn and take her over to the hen house?" said Sally. "I am pretty sure that there are plenty of eggs to pick up from those old hens today." Once again, both boys lifted up their heads, gave a nod to their mother, and then returned their focus on their plates.

"Tilly, those boys eat like there is no tomorrow," Sarah whispered to Tilly as she took her own dishes to the kitchen sink. "We are just lucky that we are able to grow enough of our own food here. And what we don't grow, we can get in town." Tilly thought to herself how different things were here in Gettysburg, different from the way things were back home. Sally's family seemed, well, happy and at peace, not having to worry about crop failure, dried up land, or a missing husband and father. Tilly, too, was anxious to see Gettysburg and looked forward to her day.

"Momma", Kathy said as she entered the kitchen," the horses have been walked, rubbed down, and fed. Can I have some breakfast now?" "I sure can honey. Here, sit down next to Sarah and you both can eat." Sally continued, "I told Sarah that after the boys take her to the hen house and collect the eggs, that you two could take the horses for a ride into town. We do need a few things at the store and you can pick them up before you come back."

By the time Sarah finished her chores with the boys, she was ready for a change of scenery. Not that the boys were a problem or anything; she just never spent too much time with any boys, let alone twins. Boys sure are different she thought to herself as she and Kathy saddled up the horses, two beautiful dark brown mares that were as cooperative as could be. As they rode into town, Sarah couldn't get over how lucky she was now in her new surroundings and felt like she had to pinch herself to make sure it wasn't a dream.

They rode past several ranches on their way to town and Sarah remarked how green everything looked and how nice the ranch houses seemed. "Yes, Gettysburg is a real nice place to live," said Kathy. "Not that I have lived anywhere else, because I haven't, but our daddy lets us know what Washington is like and how we wouldn't like big city life. He also has told us that despite the fact that the war is going on, we are in a safe place and he wants that to continue."

"Sarah, do you miss your daddy?" Kathy asked as they both came to a stop. "I sure do, Kathy, and think about him just about every day. I do wish we could hear some news about him, but I am sure that he is well." "How do you know that?" questioned Kathy. "I just do, I have a feeling, that's all," responded Sarah. As they got off their horses to look at the little lake on the right side of the road, Kathy thought she saw a tear in Sarah's eyes. "I'm sorry if I said something wrong, Sarah. I didn't mean to hurt you." "No, you didn't hurt me Kathy," Sarah said. "It just brought up the memory of saying good bye to my father when the war started and how I miss him so."

Kathy thought it best not to mention Sarah's father again, not just now, and suggested that they get back on their horses and head to town. It was not much further, and by the time they reached the general store, both girls got to know each other pretty well.

Sarah had read about Gettysburg and listened to her mother tell her about her childhood when she visited her cousin. She was not ready though to see what she saw as a landscape so unlike her own in South Carolina. In the spring, Gettysburg and the surrounding areas were sublime. Here, there were green forests and rolling hills. The pastureland was lush and filled with well- fed cattle. The ranch houses she saw were much bigger than she was used to, and they were made of stone and were indeed impressive. Just as suddenly as she began thinking about the landscape, Sarah had a thought. She hadn't seen any black people since she arrived. "Kathy, don't you have any slaves here?" Sarah asked as they continued on. "Why no, Pennsylvania is a free state Sarah. Any blacks that are here are free, many own their own properties and the ones that don't, work in town or on the ranches, although lately, we have noticed that many of them have been leaving town, a little fearful that the Confederate army might be coming to Gettysburg. Kathy continued:" I have read some about the war and what the South is fighting for Sarah. My daddy sends us the papers and some weeklies that talk about the war, who is right and who is wrong. Did you have slaves on your farm?

Sarah thought for a minute and was uncomfortable as she thought about her farm and the workers that she had known for so long. She never treated them as property, as had many of the plantation owners that she had heard of. They were just workers to her and she shared time with them without a thought of who they were or how they got to the farm in the first place. Her mother and father never talked very much about slavery in front of her and she just assumed that the way of life in South Carolina was the way all people lived. She was beginning to see things in a new light, much different from what she was used to on the farm.

Section Twenty-Seven

Joshua Gets His Orders

L ieutenant Johnson walked over to where he saw Joshua and watched as Joshua was setting out portions of whatever meat they had left in camp. There was some cornbread that Joshua had occasioned to rescue from camp the day before, some turnips and greens that he had found in the fields and some corn that some of the other soldiers had found and brought to him. To Joshua, this was a feast, compared to what he had experienced on the plantation, and especially what his unit has had the last several days. "Joshua, do you have enough food for the men?", Lieutenant Johnson asked. "Why sure, Lieutenant, just give me a little more time and all will be ready," Joshua replied. He wasn't really sure, but thought it best to be positive about the food situation. They had been having trouble of late providing food for the entire regiment, and Joshua was doing the best he could in parceling things out for the men.

Joshua thought more and more about his status with the Confederate army; he was safe, but not really safe. He didn't know where he was going, what was going to happen to him, and at his age, what the future would hold. He knew that being away from the plantation, and all its grief and despair, was a better position to be in but even with that in mind, being in the Confederate army was not much of a step up. Sure, he was not a slave anymore. Indeed, some of the soldiers even tried to befriend him while he was acting as their cook, but he did not feel free. Maybe he would never feel free, whatever that meant.

"Joshua, time is ripe. Let's get the food out to the troops," shouted Lieutenant Johnson. Joshua turned around and saw that the troops were approaching for their evening meals. He took a moment to look around at the faces of these men, some of whom looked not much older than him, with thin moustaches and skimpy beginnings of beards. Still, he was cautious, knowing how in an instant, his life could be threatened if the food was not to their liking, or if someone like Corporal Williams, took a dislike to the offerings.

He did his best to maintain a pleasant attitude; he was friendly to a fault and did his best to make sure that all the troops appreciated what food they were being given. He also did his best to make sure that his safety was protected; he knew that his position as cook could at any time be taken away if the troops, Corporal Williams, or even Lieutenant Johnson were displeased with his food or took a disliking to him for any reason. He was the only black around, and was keenly aware of how the soldiers could react should they decide to change their attitudes towards him. Surely, wartime makes it almost impossible to provide soldiers with consistently appealing meals. However, Joshua was not simply a cook in the army; he was indeed a captured slave and subject to whatever the soldiers decided was an appropriate way of showing their displeasure with his renderings. Still, he did his best to provide palatable food for his hosts.

At the same time, he thought about the next step, what he could do to leave his present position and escape. Thoughts of his conversations with Mr. Washington and about the Underground Railroad kept filtering through his mind. When might be a good time to move? Could he move? What might happen? Where would he go? These were all questions he thought about as the meal ended, and the soldiers took their time to settle in for the night.

Joshua watched as they got their tents ready and put their battle gear inside. Most of the soldiers shared a tent, using their rifles or a strong stick to hold up the canvas. Some of the soldiers began to write by the fireside, to their loved ones. Some, not knowing what was appropriate, took up their whittling, played some music on whatever musical instrument they could locate, or secretly drew from their provisions and took a swig of some beverage that may have contained some alcoholic component. Frowned upon: yes. But, experienced by many? Yes indeed!

Even Corporal Williams, who was keeping a keen eye on Joshua, took some time to be alone; to gather his thoughts, whatever they might be. Lieutenant Johnson came over to Joshua and whispered, "Joshua, tomorrow we leave for a town called Gettysburg. The rest of the boys don't know yet, but I thought I would tell you now. There might be some trouble, we don't know yet. But I suggest that you stay near the rear, with your kitchen gear, just to make sure you remain safe. We might be coming up against some opposition from the townsfolk, or any Northern troops that might be in the vicinity.

We understand that Gettysburg town has a number of businesses that could help us add to our supplies and that the town is not very well protected by Union troops. In fact, the North has no idea yet that we are headed that way. At least, that is what General Lee has told us troops. As for me, I am getting tired of just drilling, and more drilling, and am looking forward to a change."

"Thank you, Lieutenant," Joshua replied. With this information, knowing that he would be at the back of the regiment, Joshua finally thought he might have a chance. This was the first time that the troops he was with might come across the enemy. What would he do? What would they do? Would this be his chance to escape, to be a free man, or would he remain attached to this Confederate unit? For how long, he did not know!

Section Twenty-Eight

Martin Moves Towards Combat.

The train ride to Gettysburg was pretty uneventful in Martin's opinion. The train was filled with a mixture of raw recruits and seasoned veterans. Martin could overhear some of the older soldiers talking about their experiences in the war with Mexico, some years earlier, and as he listened, he could imagine himself riding with them in their quest to save Texas from the grasp of Mexico.

Martin didn't know whether their stories were true or not, for sometimes in retelling stories from the past, certain facts might be embellished to make the stories that much more interesting, or that in the retelling, they simply forgot what really happened. Nevertheless, they were still interesting for Martin to listen to. They also kept his mind from thinking about what Lieutenant Wilson said as they were given their marching orders ("there is a good chance that not everyone will be coming back.")

Suddenly, his attention shifted to the conductor in his dark, black coat and gray slacks, as he walked the aisle, swinging his watch and chain, and announcing that they were arriving at

Gettysburg. He felt excited and nervous at the same time, and was sure that the other recruits felt the same as they had talked about the War on the train ride down. He saw them look back and forth, their hands holding their rifles or haversacks tightly. They knew there would be no replacement for their personal belongings if they lost them, so they took real good care of what they had.

"Hey Ollie," Martin yelled over the crowd of soldiers to his friend who was several rows ahead of him, "meet me outside." "You got it, buddy," Ollie replied as he put on his haversack, picked up his rifle and then walked down the aisle of the train and left the car. Martin quickly followed and they both met on the train platform, they and several hundred blue suited soldiers. Martin had never heard of Gettysburg. He looked around the station and thought that it looked a lot like Westfield, another small town with that quiet, small town feel. He couldn't imagine that a battle might be fought here.

As he thought more about Gettysburg, he overheard two soldiers, new to the area, talking about the strategic value of Gettysburg. "Why, did you know that this here town, really a village of barely two thousand people, was really a hub for twelve separate roads (ten main ones and two smaller, branch roads) which spread out in every direction from the center of town, kind of like the spokes on a wheel.

These roads could take you to any number of cities, including Washington D.C., a mere seventy miles away as the crow flies," said one of the soldiers, who seemed to be older and a bit more experienced in warfare. "Yea, most of those roads are dirt roads, except a couple that are more hard- surfaced, covered with a mixture of stone and gravel, and easier for wagons to cover, especially when it was wet," he went on.

Martin wondered if that had anything to do with their reason for coming to Gettysburg in the first place. He knew from being in Westfield how important it was to have access roads to travel on when shipping armaments from the foundry to the riverboats and then down south to their ultimate destinations.

"Alright men, gather around," announced Lieutenant Wilson as the last of the soldiers got off the train. "So far, we have nothing to worry about. I have heard that a few days ago, Confederate General Early had been in town demanding some provisions from the locals, but he left soon enough and hasn't been back. He must be in the area though. Now, remember, we are guests in this town, and if anyone causes any trouble, no matter what, you will be risking a court martial and even worse, my personal wrath. We are representatives of the United States Army, and we don't want anyone to say that we weren't respectful of our hosts."

Martin and Ollie looked at each other with a sort of smile on their faces. By now they understood that the lieutenant might be a big and boisterous soldier, but deep down he was concerned about all his soldiers at heart and wished no harm to any of them. Lieutenant Wilson continued: "For now, you can use the provisions in your packs. The supply wagons will be here shortly and we can expect a big meal later on. You can refill your canteens behind the station. There is a well there, freshly dug, which has some real refreshing water for you."

Martin had some free time now, and since he didn't know whether his first letter was received by his father, he thought it a good idea to send him another. He noticed that there was a postal station not far from the train station. He found a quiet spot under a tree in the shade, took out his paper and pencil, and then crafted the following note:

Dear Father:

I hope you have received my earlier letter. I don't want you to be mad, nor do I want for you to worry about me. We just arrived in a town called Gettysburg, in Pennsylvania, and so far, there has been no activity of any kind. We most likely will be here for a while and we are to set up camp today. I have made some friends already and am getting along fine. I will try to stay in touch with you as best I can. I should probably go now. I hope that you are doing well.

Your son, Martin

With that, Martin sealed the envelope and walked over to the postal depot, deposited the letter with the postman, and then rejoined the rest of the soldiers. He felt pleased, both in writing again to his father, and also in being part of the Union army. He thought to himself that just a short time ago, he was in his bedroom, staring at the sky and wondering about his future. Now, he could stare at the sky, knowing that his future was now and what would happen tomorrow, no one could tell.

As he walked around town, he noticed how few civilian men were in town, in fact, the town seemed pretty quiet for a warm, summer day. It was hotter here than it was in Westfield, and wearing the wool uniform did not make him any more comfortable. As he took a swig of water from his canteen, Ollie tapped him on the shoulder, and commented, "Martin, did you know that Gettysburg, long before the war started, was one of the stops on that there Underground Railroad?" "Why no, Ollie," Martin replied. "I had heard of the Underground Railroad but didn't really know too much about it. "And you know what else Martin? Most of the men around here have gone off and enlisted in the Union army already!" That was why Martin didn't see too many men and the men who were not there were enlisted already, or probably home or in their businesses. He wondered whom he would be able to see while in Gettysburg and whom he would make contact with.

Section Twenty-Nine

Abigail Has a Surprise

Mrs. Handy, Robert, and Abigail climbed into the wagon, waved goodbye to Mr. Handy, as he stood on the porch of the house, and he waved back. They then began the short ride to town as each of them was thinking their own thoughts about what they would see, and whom.

"Mrs. Handy, it sure is a mighty fine day today. Look how green those fields are, and even in this heat, it is still a pleasant ride," remarked Robert, as he skillfully handled the horses. Abigail sat in the back of the wagon, and had a clear view of the rolling hills around Gettysburg, and thought of how different it was from Washington, with no hustle, no bustle, just quiet and quite beautiful. She marveled at the bluffs they passed, filled with greenery that she did not see in Washington and trees that she never saw before.

As they approached town, they noticed a large contingent of Union soldiers camped just outside of town and Abigail turned to look at the faces of all those many soldiers. She had seen this before, in the streets of Washington. When she and Rachel walked down the streets in Washington. It was a look of men and boys who had no real plan of their own, just waiting for orders from their superiors. Then she saw one young looking soldier, with his kepi off, and she thought he couldn't be much older than her.

"Mother, could we stop a minute?" Abigail turned to her mother and repeated, "Mother, can we stop a minute? There is a young soldier over there all by himself and he looks a little lonely. I noticed his companion took off a bit ago, and he was just looking out over the fields." "Now Abigail, this is not Washington, and he is not one of your vagrant pets. He has his own business to attend to," Mrs. Handy replied. Robert looked over to the soldier, looked at Abigail and suggested to Mrs. Handy that he could stay near to them, once again just to keep an eye on things, just like he had done in Washington. Mrs. Handy saw the pleading in Abigail's eyes, and said, "Well, go on then, just for a few minutes. I will go over to that general store across the street. Robert, you are in charge!" "Yes, Ma'am," Robert said in a reassuring manner.

Both Mrs. Handy and Abigail climbed out of the wagon at the same time, turned in different directions, and Robert watched as Abigail walked up to the young soldier.

"Hi, my name is Abigail. What's yours," she asked. Martin turned to her, kind of nervous like, and said, "Oh, my name is Martin. Do you live here?" "Oh no," Abigail said with a confident pose. "I live in Washington and my family is staying here on vacation. My father works for President Lincoln," she said proudly.

"Well, I don't mean to be rude or anything like that, but don't you think taking a vacation in Gettysburg might not be the safest place to be?" Martin inquired. "I hear tell that the Rebs are mighty close and there could very likely be a battle brewing soon."

Abigail replied," I know there has been talk of that, but I haven't been to town for over a week, and now that you say so, that is probably why there are so many Union troops here." Martin added: "And there are a whole lot more on the way. We have been told that General Lee and his Army of Northern Virginia are on their way to Gettysburg. As a matter of fact, one general was just here a short time ago to get some provisions for his brigade."

As Robert watched from a short distance, he couldn't help but wonder once again about his own family. Why, his son, if he were still alive, would be just about that boy's age. With that, he touched the scar on his cheek again, which reminded him of how things were, and how different his life was now.

"Miss Abigail, I think we should get ready to get back. Say your goodbyes to that young man. We should pick up your mother and get back to the house," Robert called out. "Just a minute Robert, I will be right there," responded Abigail. Abigail turned again to Martin and said, "Martin, I have to go, but here, take my address and when you leave here, if you get to Washington, you can stop at my house and say hello. You can meet my friend Rachel, and see all the critters that we are taking care of. Now you be careful!"

"Why, thank you, Abigail. I just might do that. And don't you worry about me. It will take a lot to keep this man down," Martin said half jokingly and half with a foreboding that he was beginning to feel. With that, Abigail climbed back onto the wagon, waved goodbye to Martin, as did Robert, and they turned around to go and pick up Mrs. Handy. As Martin watched them drive off, he sensed a feeling of sorrow; he was beginning to miss his father and his home, and seeing Abigail, who looked like he remembered his mother looking, well, he was definitely getting homesick for the first time. "Who was that little lady, my friend?" Ollie asked, as he gave him a poke in the side and said, "Don't tell me you have gotten a girlfriend already!" Martin pushed his hand away and said, "Aw, she just stopped to say hello, that's all," as he pushed the paper with Abigail's address deep into his pocket. Meanwhile, Robert and Abigail met Mrs. Handy in front of the store, her arms carrying several bags of groceries and other things for the house. They began to chat as Robert took the reins and urged the horses to move forward and Abigail told her mother of her visit with Martin.

"Mother, what if what Martin said was true? That the Confederates are very close to Gettysburg?" Abigail asked, somewhat nervously. Mrs. Handy sensed Abigail's insecurity, and not wanting to make her more upset, suggested, "Honey, I am sure your father wouldn't have us be here if he thought we were in danger." She gave Abigail a hug as she thought about her conversation with Mr. Handy, and his wanting them to leave. "Robert," announced Mrs. Handy, "you had better get these horses moving. I am sure that Abigail is getting hungry and it is nearly dinnertime."

"I sure will Ma'am," Robert replied, and with that, gave the whip to the horses to speed them up. "Yes, Ma'am, I can just imagine how that chicken will taste for supper tonight," Robert said reassuringly, although deep down, he also felt a bit ill at ease, considering his past in the South and the nearness of the

Confederate troops. Once again, he fingered the scar on his cheek and soon the wagon pulled up to the front of the house.

Abigail jumped down from the wagon and ran to the house, ahead of Mrs. Handy and Robert, and as she did so, Mrs. Handy turned to Robert and said, "You know Robert that Mr. Handy was advised about the troops and now that we know how close things are, we might want to think about packing up and heading back to Washington." "I would agree," he responded, and they both went into the house as Robert carried the bags behind Mrs. Handy.

Section Thirty

Sarah and Kathy Encounter Troops

A s they neared town, both Kathy and Sarah noticed a large encampment of soldiers just out beyond the train station. "I didn't know we were going to have soldiers here, not this soon," Kathy said. She added, "And look, they are all dressed in those blue uniforms. Don't they look so handsome?" Sarah wasn't sure how she felt; she had never seen a Union soldier before and even in South Carolina, she was not real sure about the Confederate soldiers, for when her daddy left, he was not in uniform, but merely in his farmer's garb. "Kathy, I don't think it is a such a good idea to stay around here. Who knows what is going to happen," Sarah remarked.

"Well, let's go to the post office and see if the postman can give us some information. We still have time, but we probably shouldn't stay too long. We will have to go home and tell our mothers," Kathy cautioned. As they guided their horses up to the hitching posts in front of the post office, well, it was actually a small part of the larger general store, they got down, tied up the reins, and then walked in. They saw a small crowd of adults talking and as they approached them, one lady turned and said to them: "Girls, what are you doing here? Haven't you heard the news?" Sarah spoke up and said, "No, what news Miss?" The lady replied, "Some Reb soldiers were just here a bit ago and were looking for provisions. They mentioned that they were encamped not too far from town. And now, we have Union soldiers just arriving. I am afraid we might see some trouble here pretty soon. I, myself, will be leaving with my family tomorrow to get away before something nasty happens. Why, even the postmaster, Mr. Buehler, has left town leaving his wife, Fannie, and their children to fend for themselves. I don't know why they didn't go with him, but he must have heard something mighty frightening to him."

Kathy and Sarah looked at each other with surprise on their faces, thanked the lady for the information and walked out of the post office. As they did so, they noticed one lone soldier, not much older looking than them, sitting off by himself and writing something. "Let's go see what he is doing," Kathy stated.

"I don't know, Kathy. I am sure he is there by himself for a reason, and probably doesn't want to be disturbed. Besides, he is a soldier, even if he looks kind of young, and we are just girls," Sarah explained. They watched for a moment and then the soldier got up, and began walking towards them with an envelope in his hand, headed for the post office. As he approached them, he tipped his kepi, nodded and said hello. Both girls were speechless; then Kathy said, "hello." That was it; he kept walking up to the post office and then the girls kind of giggled together and then were embarrassed at each other and decided to get back on their horses and head back to the farm and let Tilly and Sally know the news. As they left, both girls looked back over their shoulders and noticed the soldier looking at them. He then waived and as he did so, they each turned around at the same time, saw the other blushing, and then turned away, each giggling to each other.

Before they headed home though, Sarah wanted to get a better look of the town and convinced Kathy to show her around some more. They were not aware of how close the war was to them; they were children, not familiar with why troops were beginning to gather on both sides of town. They also lost track of time and before they knew it, dusk was settling in and Kathy advised that rather than try to ride back home, they could stay in town with one of her friends, Hannah Barr, who lived with her mother, Agnes. Her mother and Agnes' mother had been friends for years, and Kathy had often stayed with Hannah before. Her mother was comfortable with that arrangement and often, Kathy would not even let her mother know. Sally was well aware of that and after time, she was not concerned, knowing that Kathy would always come back the next day. Besides, she had enough on her hands with her two sons.

They approached the Barr house, and Mrs. Barr invited them in. "Now girls, I am so glad you are here. Troops are gathering as we speak and word has it that fighting could start at any time. Kathy, we will have to get word to your mother that you are here. For now, you should stay with us until we get a better idea of what is about to happen." Mrs. Barr called out to Hannah, who was in the cellar to come up and see who was here. When

Hannah came up from the cellar, with her arms filled with a bag of flour and other provisions, she let out a yelp, dropped them all on the floor and ran to Kathy. "Oh Kathy, I am so glad to see you," she said. She then turned, saw Sarah standing alone, and said: "And who do we have here?" Kathy replied, "This is Sarah, she is visiting us from South Carolina for a spell. Our mothers are cousins." "Nice to meet you Sarah," offered Hannah, and the girls shook hands in typical fashion for two strangers. "We were just about getting ready to make dinner; want to give us a hand?" Hannah asked. Kathy replied, "Sure, just show us what to do." And with that, the two girls prepared to spend the night in Gettysburg, not knowing what the next day, the first day of July, would bring for them all.

Section Thirty-One

Joshua Faces His Destiny

Joshua was always a good listener. From the early days on the plantation, where he would listen to his momma and Mr. Washington, and, well, even evil Mr. Potts, Joshua was like a sponge soaking up water. He was also very polite, another trait that his mother encouraged as he was growing up. He found information interesting, even exciting, and now that he was with the Confederate army, he listened more, finding out about the War, its history over the last two years, the leaders on both sides, facts and figures about the battles, who won, who lost, and so on. Lieutenant Johnson took Joshua under his wing, not so much for his protection, for surely that was one outcome, but also because he could tell that Joshua was intelligent, and tried to make good decisions and stay out of trouble. It was more or less a teacher-student relationship, or as close as one could be, given their differing backgrounds and the circumstances they were under.

He had learned that his brigade had joined up with Brigadier General J. Johnson Pettigrew, a respected and experienced general, and one of General Lee's most trusted generals, and that they were marching on to a town called Gettysburg. Joshua felt a mix of excitement and fear all at the same time. He was not in the front lines, and was not allowed to carry a gun, but he could see and read pretty clearly the faces of the soldiers around him. While he prepared food for meals he was somewhat relieved that he was not the only cook, but one of many. He again listened to the stories of the battles that he was not a part of. He learned that information passes quickly among the troops, some exaggerated and some very real. When he found out how many soldiers from various directions were approaching Gettysburg, he was amazed that that many soldiers could be assembled in one place and at one time.

"Joshua, we are very close to a real battle with those Union soldiers," Lieutenant Johnson told Joshua as they were talking together over some dinner. Lieutenant Johnson often sat with Joshua while eating. He enjoyed the boy's company and marveled at how skilled Joshua was in food preparation, something he also had interest in, but given the present circumstances, he had to refrain from.

"Why just yesterday, I heard that General Early and his troops went to Gettysburg to pick up some supplies, including flour, meat, wearing apparel and barrels of whiskey, and then left immediately. We also heard that Union troops came into town shortly thereafter. We do know through our scouts that most of the able bodied young men from Gettysburg had already enlisted in the Union army, leaving mostly older men and women, young boys and girls and those who were not allowed to enlist for various reasons. Now, Joshua, I want you to know that in the next day or so, we might see some heavy fighting, nothing like what you have seen up till now. I care for you and don't want to see you hurt or possibly killed. So, I want you to stay back with the mules and the wagons if we are called to move out. Promise me that you will do that."

Joshua could see the intensity in the Lieutenant's eyes, and knew by now that the Lieutenant was being sincere. "Yes, sir," Joshua replied with the same intensity. "I will do as you say."

As the sun rose on the morning of July 1, and the day began, Joshua started his usual chores around the camp and looked after the stores of food for the troops. He began to hear the sound of gunfire, but it was more than just occasional gunfire. He heard gunfire on the plantation from time to time. This sound was much louder, and it sounded like a great many guns being shot. Joshua would later learn that Union General Buford's cavalry had made contact with the Confederate infantry to the west of Gettysburg, at a place called McPherson's Ridge. He now knew that a full battle was inevitable and that his brigade, led by Lieutenant Johnson under the command of General Pettigrew, was well underway to join the battle and move closer to town. Still, he stayed back, following the command of his Lieutenant. He could not imagine what was going to happen next, nor could he envision the possibility of mass destruction that could occur, on both sides.

As the day progressed, and Joshua could hear the shelling going on, he could not help but think about his role. "I know that I am supposed to stay here," he said out loud, and no one else who stayed back with him had heard him as he spoke, "but what if I can be of help?" He looked around, and saw some of the other cooks and some of the injured men sitting around the wagons and not paying any attention to him. He made his decision; he had to move. He gathered up some gear, threw his haversack over his shoulder, picked up a rifle that had been left behind as the brigade took off, and slowly, very slowly, with his head down and his cap lowered over his forehead, snuck out of camp, and headed to where the sound of battle was the greatest.

As he moved, he could smell the smell of the weaponry. The hot, muggy air kept that smell, and the smoke of gunfire, hanging in the air, making it hard to take a deep breath. He poured water from his canteen down his throat, and wiped his face as best he could with his sleeve. He never did get accustomed to wearing a Confederate uniform. Though it was hot and heavy and made it difficult for him to move quickly, that was all he had to wear now. He didn't like the way his boots fit either, but he knew that wearing those heavy boots was safer than going barefoot in this terrain. As he continued, he saw Confederate forces enter the town and could see some young boys climb onto some of the rooftops to watch the action take place.

He found himself a spot that was away from the gunfire, but close enough so he could see the troops, both North and South, at various times during the day, coming through town. He wasn't sure what to do now; he didn't want to join the fray, he didn't want to let Lieutenant Johnson know he disobeyed him, but he wanted to do something. He couldn't just stay in that one spot forever. He could see some of the townsfolk running and climbing down into their cellars to avoid the conflict.

By nightfall, the Confederate troops occupied the town, and the Union soldiers retreated for the night. By then, he, too, found a cellar in one of the houses whose wooden door was open and climbed in. Apparently, the owners of the house were gone and fortunately, the cellar was quiet and appeared empty. He crawled way back in the corner, into the darkness, covered himself with some burlap sacks and immediately fell asleep, unaware whether anyone else might have been in the cellar.

Section Thirty-Two

Martin Faces Combat for the First Time

As June 30th ended, and with the coming of nightfall, Martin, Ollie and the rest of the soldiers under Lieutenant Wilson's command were ordered to go west of Gettysburg and join the regiments of other Union commanders. They now knew how close Lee's armies were to Gettysburg, and sought to convene and determine their next maneuvers. By now, Martin was so anxious to become involved in the warfare that Ollie held onto him and said, "Martin, I don't know why you are so determined to move into this battle. You have already heard about the skirmishes that took place today; are you sure you want to test your marksmanship against the army of the South?" Martin turned to Ollie and replied," Ollie, I don't know what happened to you? We were just talking yesterday about taking part in this battle, and now you seem to be more reluctant to enter into the fray." "Martin," Ollie responded with a kind of sad look on his face, "I haven't ever killed a man before. Oh, maybe some deer or birds, but really, shooting another man, I am not real sure." "Ollie, get yourself together," shouted Martin. "We are here to fight a war, and you can't back out now. It's too late, and besides, the rebels are just around the corner."

Martin let it go; he knew how upset Ollie was and even though he was younger, he did not carry the same fear or suspicion that Ollie did. They settled in for the night, outside of Gettysburg. Martin reached into his pocket and remembered the piece of paper that Abigail had given him. As he fingered the paper, he said to himself quietly, "I will definitely have to find her in Washington, once I get there." He lay back on his blanket and once again, looked up at the stars, like he used to do at home. He had come a long way from Westfield, life was different now, and his life had definitely taken a turn. He again thought of his meeting with Abigail, and wondered what her life was like in Washington. The more he thought, the more comfortable he became, lying on his blanket, for the time feeling safe and sound.

As he awoke the next morning, Martin was startled by the sound of gunfire. It was July 1, and the battle had begun, with both sides coming into Gettysburg, and moving back and forth, first the Confederates, then the Union soldiers. Gettysburg had become a seesaw with the opposing troops like children on either end. The shooting was constant and as his regiment moved, dead and wounded were found everywhere. Martin passed over bodies, some hardly recognizable due to their wounds, he knew that this would not be an easily won battle. As the day wore on, with Ollie by his side, and among the many other Union soldiers, he heard the bugle call to retreat and leave the town for the day. The

Confederates had just too strong of a hold on the area and his commanders did not want to risk the loss of any more lives.

Although Martin had fired his rifle often, he was not sure whether he had actually hit, let alone killed anyone. He was not close enough to the enemy to tell. He thought for a moment that maybe that was okay. Maybe he wouldn't have to kill anyone after all. As his regiment found safe ground, and each soldier found a spot to rest, Martin cleaned his weapon and prepared to hunker in for the night. He could smell the smell of spent shells, while smoke still spread through the evening sky.

He also thought about his home, his father, and most recently, the girls he had seen; Abigail, with her servant, Robert, all prim and proper, riding in their wagon, and then, later, Sarah and Kathy, riding like cowgirls into and out of town on their horses. How strange this War is, he thought to himself, as he looked over to Ollie, who had already fallen asleep, his rifle firmly positioned across his chest. Here we are, all uniformed and taking part in a war, and there are so many others, including young people, who are just here and have no real part in this war.

The night was still; both sides had taken time to recoup, to count their losses, to plan for the next day and get some needed rest. In town, the civilians were able to come out of hiding, assist the wounded the best they could and count their own blessings that they were saved from injury, or worse. They could see the bullet-ridden buildings, the bodies of some soldiers who were not fortunate enough to survive the day's battle, and the aftermath of the day's battle. They salvaged what they could. They even helped bring some wounded soldiers into their homes and then took care of their own needs as best they could. They also knew that this battle was not yet over. Many, if not all of the residents of Gettysburg, were sympathizers of the North. As such, the civilians, mostly women, dressed the Union soldiers that they found in civilian clothes so that the Confederates who occupied Gettysburg that night would not discover whom or where they were.

Martin lay there, in his bedroll, and despite being physically worn out from the day's events, he could not sleep. His body was tired, indeed, but his mind was still racing. He decided to get up and knowing that the fighting had stopped, he wanted to see what the area was like at night. He was a soldier, but he was still a youth, filled with youthful wonder. It was still warm, being July, and he didn't need his overcoat, so he wrapped it in his blanket, put his kepi at the top, and for all intents and purposes it could have looked like he was sleeping there. He then began to wander about, looking down from the ridge where the Union soldiers were encamped, and wondered what the next day would bring.

Section Thirty-Three

Abigail and Her Family Leave Gettysburg

Fortunately, the train out of Gettysburg was still running, so after they made the necessary arrangements to leave, including thanking Mr. Sweeney for his help, Mrs. Handy, Mr. Handy, Abigail, and Robert were all able to gather at the train station before they had seen any actual fighting in or around Gettysburg.

"John," inquired Mrs. Handy as they boarded the train, "what have you heard from Washington?" She was careful not to let Abigail, or even Robert, hear her. "The wire I got said that the Confederate troops are just outside of Gettysburg, and that our troops are building beyond, but the Confederates don't know that yet. My guess is that in the next couple of days, there will be some severe fighting outside of town. Both sides want to limit the involvement of the civilians, but in war, you can never be too sure what might happen. It is good that we are leaving now. We should be home before July 1, if all goes well with our transfers.

We can follow the news of the war when we get there," he replied. With that, Mr. Handy sat back in his seat on the train and looked out the window, not letting the others know of his concern.

The train trip back to Washington was relatively quick and uneventful thought Abigail. As she got back to her house, she noticed how the streets were not as filled as they were before she left. "Mother, look how empty the streets are," she pointed while talking to her mother. "I know dear, most of the troops have been mustered up and have left for battle. We left Gettysburg not a moment too soon," she said convincingly. They all went into the house, leaving Robert to carry the heavier bags, a role he was quite familiar with.

"I will speak to Mr. Lincoln tomorrow, dear, and see if he can give me some additional information. I know now that we are safe here in Washington, and at least Abigail has her friend, Rachel, once again. Why, they can even resume their animal saving efforts and if they want, they can use the spare room," John said with a smile on his face. "Oh, John, that would be just wonderful, "Mrs. Handy exclaimed as she gave her husband a hug, happy they were home.

Abigail sat on her bed looking out her window waiting for Rachel to come over, and thought about the boy she had met in Gettysburg. She wondered how he was doing and whether any harm would come to him. She also wondered if he would keep her name and address as well!

"Oh Rachel," Abigail shouted excitedly as Rachel came into her room. "How happy I am to see you." Rachel rushed over to her and they both hugged, with Rachel saying, " Abigail, you have to tell me every little thing about your trip to Gettysburg."

"I want to hear all the details." "Now just wait a minute, Rachel, I just got back in town. Can you give me some time to gather my thoughts? Don't be so anxious. I know you are excited, as am I." After Abigail sat down, as did Rachel, she began, "First, Gettysburg is a very small town. A little over two thousand people, but with the war going on, and many of the menfolk gone, it was almost like a ghost town compared to Washington."

Rachel then cut her off and said," and did you see any boys, you know, any boys our age?" "Promise me you won't say a word to anyone?" Abigail offered. "Of course not, cross my heart," said Rachel, and she took her hand to cross her heart. "Well, I did meet this boy, actually he was a soldier, but he was very young. We talked a bit, and I gave him my name and address and told him that if he comes to Washington, to look me up." "You didn't!" said Rachel rather excitedly, and then Abigail motioned her to be quiet.

"My parents don't know about this and I don't want them to be asking me any questions. You know how they can be!" She continued, "I met him just after he first arrived in Gettysburg. He was alone and I walked up to him and we had a real brief conversation." With that, they both agreed to put that little issue aside, and went downstairs to see what their next plan of action would be, now that they were going to back in the business of saving the animal world in Washington!

Section Thirty-Four

Sarah Gets Lost

On the morning of July 1, Sarah, Kathy, and Hannah woke to something that was so unfamiliar to them, something not within their realm of knowledge. Because they were living on the northwest side of town, they and their neighbors heard the first sounds of battle. For the most part, it took place outside the town limits, and some townspeople gathered along Seminary Ridge to see what was going on. During the course of the day, first Union troops, and later, Confederate troops, would march through town. Late in the afternoon, Union officers warned the residents to stay inside, that gunfire was going on and their safety could not be ensured. Mrs. Barr and the girls stayed inside all day, listening to the gunfire and even seeing soldiers, either wounded or worse, in the streets. By nightfall, Confederate troops occupied the town, while the Union troops retreated and regrouped outside of town.

"What are we going to do now?" asked the girls, almost in unison. They looked at each other and then Mrs. Barr spoke up: "Girls, we have to stay inside now. We don't know what those troops are going to do and we don't want to take any chances. I recall from earlier in this war how some civilians who ventured into the fray were hit by stray gunfire, and I certainly don't want that to happen to any of you. Fortunately, we have a passageway down to the cellar that we can go to if need be, without having to go outside." That is exactly what they did once the sun began to set and the streets became quiet.

As the girls settled in, Sarah thought about her momma; what would she think? Surely, they could hear the sounds of battle and she was sure her momma would be worried, no matter what Sally would say to try to calm her. At the same time, her curiosity, and her sense of adventure, not hampered by the warnings of Mrs. Barr, made her restless. On her farm, she was not one to stay put; if she heard anything unusual, she would go outside to see what it was. But this was not South Carolina, and certainly not a quiet farm, far away from possible danger.

Sarah waited until everyone had fallen asleep. She couldn't hear anything outside. The shooting had subsided and there were no more troops scavenging for supplies, as far as she could tell as she climbed the cellar stairs. She looked out the window and still, she saw nothing. She was intrigued. She felt like she had to see what had happened. She slowly opened the front door, listened for anything that might resemble movement, but heard and saw nothing. She left the house, began slowly walking down the street, looking back and forth, making sure not to make any sound. The dirt road muffled the sounds of her boots, and absorbed her every step. Should she continue? Should she go back? She thought to herself. What would father do?

She walked slowly, noticing that the cellar doors belonging to the houses were closed. The windows of the houses were covered with those heavy lace curtains she often admired in the store in town, concealing in part the insides of the houses. Of course, there were no candles burning, no oil lamps lit, so moonlight was her guide as she walked down the street. Suddenly, she heard voices behind her, not close, but distinct. They were coming from somewhere between her and the Barr house. She could not go back that way, so she hurried forward, careful to watch her steps and not make any noise as she darted from house to house. As the voices got louder, she decided to take whatever cover she could find. Up ahead, she saw a cellar door that for whatever reason was still open. She moved quickly, flung herself through the opening and not bothering to use the steps, jumped down into the darkness. Unfortunately, as she did so, she hit her head on one of the beams supporting the floor of the house, and fell to the floor, onto a pile of burlap bags, losing consciousness immediately.

Section Thirty-Five

Joshua Discovers Sarah, and More

"What was that?" Joshua said out loud. He had been sleeping and was awakened by a loud noise. At first, as he was coming out of a deep sleep, he thought it was a shot being fired. He sat up instinctively, still covered with burlap, when, despite the darkness of the cellar, he could make out a figure not far from him. It was not moving, and it definitely was not a soldier, so he slowly got up and kneeled toward what he soon realized was a young girl, lying down on her face. He touched her arm, but she did not move. He couldn't see very well, and then remembered that he had some old matches in his haversack. Reaching in, he found two, then struck one against the beam next to him. It lit up the cellar enough for him to see that it was a girl, and he also saw that she had some blood on the side of her face. He looked around and saw some old, discarded candles nearby, reached for one and lit it with the match that was just about ready to die out. He lifted the candle and placed it near her face and saw that she was a white girl, and the blood had come from the side of her head. There was not a lot of blood, but she wasn't moving.

Joshua then shook her a bit but she didn't move. He then shook her a little harder and he heard a moan coming from the girl. She began to move a bit and turned her head to the side and instantly saw Joshua's candle lit face staring at her. "Who are you?" she yelled out. Joshua didn't want to have her sound travel up the cellar door and onto the street, so he put his hand over her mouth. "Shush," he cautioned, "there may be soldiers wandering the streets up above and I don't want to have anyone know I am here."

"Don't you touch me," Sarah said through her muffled voice. "I will not hurt you, I promise," Joshua whispered. "Please don't say anything more until I finish talking," Joshua responded. Then he began telling her his story, and how he came to be in the same cellar with her.

As he spoke, Sarah became more relaxed; she sensed a certain kindness coming from Joshua and wasn't afraid, and the more Joshua spoke, the more comfortable she found herself. She now began to feel the pain in her head though, and Joshua could tell she was in distress. "Here, let's pour some water on this cloth and wipe your head," Joshua offered, as he dipped the cloth into a pan of water on the floor, and then wiped the blood from her forehead. A large bump was developing on the side of her face and as she sat up, she said, "Ow, that really hurts." "You must have hit your head as you came into the cellar, and then fell down here," Joshua stated. "What is your name?" "Sarah," she replied, "and yours?" "I am called Joshua" and he sat down next to her. He wiped her forehead again, and then, suddenly, they both heard footsteps and turned to see booted feet, then legs, then the body of a uniformed soldier climbing down the stairs.

"Who is down here?" Martin shouted. He could see the dimly lit candle but not the faces of anyone. Joshua was too scared to speak up so Sarah did: "My name is Sarah and I am here with Joshua," she shouted. Martin looked over to where he thought the voice was coming from and saw Joshua's Confederate uniform and how close he was to Sarah and yelled out, "you, stay away from that girl. I have a gun here and if you move a hair, I will put you away." He had not yet seen the color of Joshua's skin, but just reacted to the uniform. He did not have his rifle with him and he cursed to himself for not having it, and for wandering off in the first place.

He took off his hat (for after leaving his Kepi at the campsite, he found another on the side of the road, and thought it might come in handy) to wipe his face, as it was stifling hot in the cellar, and then Sarah recognized him as the young soldier she had seen earlier. "Hey, I know you," said Sarah, and with that she stood up as best she could and Martin also recognized her. Joshua also stood up and for the first time, Martin saw Joshua's skin color, and assuming the worst, once again spoke up with an authoritarian tone, "I said don't move. Now, get away from that girl and go sit in that corner with your hands behind you."

"Wait, shouted Sarah, wanting to make herself heard. "He was helping me." With that, Sarah related how she got to the cellar in the first place, her fall, and how Joshua had helped her. Martin relaxed as well and let Joshua explain to him, just as he had explained to Sarah, how he found himself in the cellar.

As Martin now was looking at Sarah's wound, all three youngsters sat around not really knowing what to do next. He patted her head, realizing that the wound was not real bad. He had seen such injuries at the foundry, and knew that she would be okay. "Please don't say anything about my being here," Joshua spoke up." "If I am caught, I am sure I will be shot, either as a deserter, or because I am black sitting here with two white people." "Now hold on there, Joshua," Martin stated. "I am no fan of hurting anyone, but we have a serious situation here. Let me think a little."

After what seemed like forever to Joshua and Sarah, Martin spoke up: "I have to get back to my brigade because they don't know I am gone yet. You two stay here. The fighting has stopped for now, but it will start up again in the morning and the safest place for you both is right here." Then Sarah spoke up, "Martin, I was staying with a family not too far from here. It is the Barr house, just down the road. If you can get there before daylight and let Mrs. Barr know about us, I am sure she can help." Sarah described the house in as much detail as she could, and Martin thought about it briefly, and then agreed to follow Sarah's instructions.

He climbed up out of the cellar, and seeing that the streets were now empty, headed over to the Barr house. He knocked softly at first, then a little harder. He then found some small stones and threw them at the window. He heard footsteps and then the door opened and Mrs. Barr was there. As he was wearing a Union uniform, she was not disturbed, just curious. "What in the world?" she said out loud. Martin asked her to be quiet, stepped inside the house at Mrs. Barr's direction, and then explained to her the earlier events. "Well young man, I guess I can go down there and do the best I can," she replied. With that, Martin took off back to his brigade.

Mrs. Barr got some blankets and a lantern and walked slowly down the street to the open cellar, found both Joshua and Sarah huddled in the corner, and hurried them back to her house. She washed Sarah's forehead and seeing that the injury was not too serious, she put her in her own room, came back and gave Joshua some fresh clothes so he wouldn't have to continue wearing the Confederate colors, and then led him down to her own cellar, admonishing him to stay there until she could figure out what to do next. Joshua said, "Thank you Mrs. Barr. This is really kind of you," and then for the third time this evening, Joshua told Mrs. Barr his story before he, too, fell asleep.

Section Thirty-Six

Martin Welcomes Joshua into His Brigade

"Lieutenant, Lieutenant, please wake up," whispered Martin, as he tugged on Lieutenant Wilson's sleeve. "I have to tell you something real important."

The lieutenant woke up with a start, shook his head side to side and said," Martin, what in tarnation is going on? Have you seen a ghost or something?" "Of course not," replied Martin. "Maybe something even worse," he stammered! "Well, out with it boy," the lieutenant said.

"I guess I probably should not have done this, but, I took a walk a little earlier, and…" "You what?" Lieutenant Wilson cut him off, now sitting up straight so that he towered over Martin, even while sitting. Martin filled him in on what happened earlier and the predicament that Joshua was in. The lieutenant thought a bit, rubbed his hand on his beard, now matted due to sleep and said, "Martin, what you did to begin with was wrong, drastically wrong. Not only did you disobey an order to remain in camp, but you risked your life for a walk!" Lieutenant Wilson continued, "I know you are young and inexperienced, but there is no excuse for what you did. Why, you could have gotten all of us in trouble if you were captured, or even seen coming back to camp. I could even have you court-martialed for what you did. Still, what you did was a real humanitarian thing, and I can't forget that. Now, let's get down to brass tacks."

They talked for a few minutes and the lieutenant agreed to go back into town to get Joshua, and bring him to his brigade. It was still dark and the streets were quiet as Martin and Lieutenant Wilson scanned the area for the Barr house. Finally finding the Barr house, Lieutenant Wilson knocked on the door and introduced himself to Mrs. Barr. She invited the lieutenant and Martin into her parlor and then called for Joshua to come up from the cellar. He did so rather reluctantly, for he did not know what was going to happen next. As he entered the room, seemingly in a cowardly manner, head down and hands folded in front of him, Lieutenant Wilson could sense the fear in the boy, and thought what he should do. Surely, he can't go back to the Confederates, and he really didn't need another young man in his brigade, although there were already a number of freed or escaped slaves that were with him, so he decided to allow Joshua to stay with them.

"Now Joshua," the lieutenant said in a professorial manner, looking down on Joshua as if he were a young schoolboy standing before a seasoned teacher, "since you have experience as a cook, I reckon you can stay on with us. We can always use another cook here, not that we have that many provisions, but you can help rest of the other men."

Joshua thought he had heard a miracle, now that he was taking part in the war on the side of the Union forces, the side that wanted to abolish slavery. "Martin, take Joshua and get him another uniform, this time a Union uniform; he is now one of us!" boasted Lieutenant Wilson.

The boys looked at each other, but Joshua quickly turned away; he didn't want Martin to see the tears in his eyes, not tears of sadness, but tears of happiness. He was safe now, and on the side that accepted him for what he was, a simple, young boy who by the grace of God had a black skin instead of a white one.

As the sun came up on the second day of July, Lieutenant Wilson called for his men to gather and plan out their day, as many more brigades of Union soldiers were coming to Gettysburg. Joshua was to stay behind, just like he had done the day before when he was still part of the Confederate army. The troops were planning to encounter some heavy artillery fire from the Confederate army.

As expected, the fighting continued, but not until late afternoon. Then, all hell broke loose as both sides battled hand to hand until the evening, when the Confederates chose to retreat and regroup. This gave the Union soldiers time to do the same, and they spread over the battlefield to gather up the wounded and/or dead, as fast as they could, before being seen and possibly fired upon by the Confederates. Martin helped, along with his friend Ollie, and both had a difficult time inspecting the bodies of those that were not able to come back. "Martin," Ollie spoke up as he walked in between bodies of soldiers that were scattered all around him, " I can't believe what we are seeing here. There are just too many bodies to handle, and too few of us."

"I know Ollie," Martin replied. He, too, was overwhelmed by the sheer numbers of soldiers lying around, let alone having to examine the injuries and see all the blood and horrendous scenes of death caused by the Confederate shelling and shooting. He wondered if the Confederate soldiers who were wandering the fields, just like them, had the same reactions. He could see them at a distance, and thought that we are all human beings and must have the same kinds of feelings. "Ollie," Martin remarked, "if we ever get out of this alive..." "Wait, Martin," Ollie interrupted, "we are going to survive this battle, and the war, so don't start with that." "I was just saying, Ollie, that when the war is over, I hope we don't ever have to see this kind of thing again." Martin then changed the subject and advised Ollie that a young lady was shot while in her kitchen making bread. It was a stray bullet that had passed through the door of her house and hit her. Her name was Jenny Wade. What did she do to cause her to die? It's just not fair! Both Ollie and Martin then became silent, as they continued to walk among the casualties of war, but then Ollie added, sympathetically: "Life is not fair, Martin."

In addition to searching for the wounded, the Union soldiers used the cover of darkness and quietude to strengthen their defenses. Additional artillery was brought into place to provide valuable cross fire for the next day when the Confederates would surely attack again as more troops had joined Martin's and the other brigades that surrounded the town of Gettysburg.

Section Thirty-Seven

Pickett's Charge

July 3, 1863. The day began very hot, with a glaring sun and no clouds to provide cover for the soldiers. Martin and Ollie, along with the many soldiers among them, prepared for battle. They were positioned high on a ridge, and could see across the open fields to the forests beyond, barely a mile away, where the Confederate army had camped for the night. Martin did not know what was going to happen next, nor did he know of any special orders, other than to hold the ridge.

Soon, a little past one in the afternoon, there began a barrage of cannon fire that he had never heard the likes of before. A long line of Confederate cannons began firing across the field with a deafening roar, over one hundred and twenty pieces, of various sizes, and thus began the bombardment, which was followed in response by a barrage of approximately eighty Union guns, from a point called Cemetery Ridge, where Martin and his troops were stationed.

After the guns stopped, there lay in the still air a pall of smoke so thick, and so filled with the stench of gunpowder, that

Martin could not believe what he was seeing. He reached over to Ollie and jabbed him in the soldier: "Ollie, look, look over there," as he pointed across the field at the edge of the woods. "Here they come."

As they both watched, they could see a mile-long line of Confederate troops slowly leaving the woods, marching in unison. Why, they were headed directly at Cemetary Ridge where Martin and Ollie were situated! They heard Lieutenant Wilson shout out, "Men, hold your fire until they are close enough to make a good shot. I believe that they will march like that for a while, as that is their style, but once you hear that Rebel yell, prepare yourselves." On the Confederate side, General Lee had amassed his forces under a number of generals, including George Pickett, who would forever be remembered as the leader of Pickett's Charge, the last and deciding charge that day.

The Confederate troops kept advancing and upon reaching Emmitsburg Road, the Union artillery opened up, firing directly at the advancing Confederate troops with great precision. The Confederate cannons, located behind their troops, were silent; either they were out of ammunition, or they feared that they might hit their own troops. Martin and Ollie readied themselves, took up their rifles and began to shoot. Standing next to each other, they aimed and shot, aimed and shot, and aimed and shot again. Suddenly, Ollie was hit and fell backward.

Martin looked down and knew that Ollie would not get back up. A bullet had hit him just below the shoulder where Martin knew his heart was. Martin turned, both with sadness and a determination for revenge, but as he did so, he, too, was hit, this time in the right arm. He spun around with the force of the bullet, and all he could see was black as he lost consciousness and fell to the ground.

The battle continued in the open field. Some of the Confederate forces had gotten as far as Cemetery Ridge but they were finally repulsed, and began to retreat. As they did so, many of the Union soldiers stood up and cheered and shouted, "Fredericksburg, Fredericksburg" to commemorate the Union defeat at the Battle of Fredericksburg. With that, the Confederate troops, pulled back, picking up as many of the wounded as they could. General Lee, standing back at the edge of the field, surveyed the massacre through his binoculars, and couldn't help but feel regret. He took the blame for the loss upon himself, stating to General Pickett, who also was at the back of the field, "this was all my fault." General Pickett and others tried to reassure General Lee that it was not his fault. This was yet another casualty of war. The troops then continued en masse, and the Union army, also worn out and desperate to take care of the dead and wounded, did not resume fighting.

Joshua, who was still back in camp, would never know that among the casualties that day was the entire brigade under the command of Lieutenant Johnson, as well as Lieutenant Johnson himself, his savior from that first day he was found in the woods after running away from the plantation.

Section Thirty-Eight

Sarah and Tilly Are Shocked at Their Findings

The front door opened and as Sally and Tilly walked onto the porch, they saw Sarah and Kathy jump from a wagon and run down the path towards them. "Oh mother," shouted Kathy, "I can't believe we are finally home." As Sarah and Kathy ran up onto the porch, both women wiped their eyes with their aprons and accepted the girls' hugs willingly. "We didn't know what was going to happen to us," said Sarah. "Girls, girls, calm down a bit," remarked Sally. "Here, have a glass of lemonade and sit here with us. We want to hear the whole story."

As the girls related the happenings of the last several days, both women thought quietly to themselves about how grateful they were that the girls were back. Tilly looked at Sarah's head, checking that the she was indeed all right. "Sarah, how does your head feel?" "It's a little sore, Momma, but I am fine" responded Sarah. "Don't worry!" As they spoke, the man in the wagon waived a friendly good bye and then turned the wagon around and headed back to town.

"Mother," added Kathy, "there are so many men in town who are wounded and need help. There aren't nearly enough nurses or doctors to help, and we heard that Dorothea Dix is even in town helping nurse the soldiers. She is well known for starting up a number of hospitals and nursing centers and Lord knows this town can certainly use all the help it can get. There are Union and Confederate soldiers alike, and people are even taking them into their homes to help out. There is even a temporary hospital starting to open outside of town.

The girls looked at each other, nodded, and then Sarah spoke up: "Momma, I know how much you helped take care of our help on the farm when they had illnesses or when old Tom fell from the barn loft and broke his leg. I bet you could be a great help in town now." Tilly looked at Sally, who had a smile on her face and said, "you go ahead Tilly. See what you can do. I will stay here with Kathy and the boys. I am sure that Sarah would like to help as well." "Can I, Momma, can I?" asked Sarah with such excitement that she could not say no. "I am sure that the town of Gettysburg can use two more helpers," Tilly offered. "But first, you girls need some rest. We can go back in a couple of days and see what we can do." With that, they all marched into the house. As it was lunchtime, and the boys were already pounding on the table with a fury that only two boys could muster up when they were hungry, Tilly and Sally began to make lunch while Sarah and Kathy washed up.

"I am sure things will be safe in town, Tilly," said Sally, as she was cutting the tomatoes on the wooden table, which was also covered with slices of fresh bread and some cold cuts. "I am not concerned with safety, Sally, I am just concerned for Sarah. All that bloodshed…"

"Hey now," Sally interrupted, "this is real life dear, and the sooner that Sarah faces the truth, the more she will understand and appreciate the efforts of these young men, on both sides. I know it is not pleasant, but they do need the help." Tilly responded, "I guess you are right. We can go tomorrow, as long as you can take us." "Surely I will," said Sally. "I need to see how things are in town anyway, and also thank Mrs. Barr for watching over the girls. I also want to hear more about those boys. Imagine, a black boy dressed in Confederate garb meeting a boy from New York who was a Union soldier, both of them a long way from home."

Riding into town the next day was no easy task for any of them. They saw fences and crops that had been broken and trampled on, animals lying in the fields or scampering away, unbridled and many soldiers, both dead and wounded, lying in the fields and being cared for by the women from town, as well as some of the older citizens who had not gone off to war. They rode past the general hospital, if you could call it that; it was an old barn that had been converted into what you could call a hospital, with people running in and out, carrying whatever supplies they could find.

"Let's stop here a minute, Sally," said Tilly. "I want…" Suddenly, Tilly's face turned pale and she stood rock solid. "What is the matter, Tilly," Sally said. "Tilly, Tilly, what is the matter?" she repeated, as she took Tilly by the arm. "I, I, there are some men over there, some Confederate soldiers. See them?

There, by the side of the barn. I have to…" With that, Tilly began to walk, then run to the group. They were being guarded by a Union soldier who saw Tilly approaching and said, "Stop there young lady. These here are captured rebel soldiers, our prisoners, and we can't let anyone near them, except for the doctors or nurses."

"JOHN," Tilly screamed, as she pushed the soldier's arm aside. "JOHN!" She ran, and the man she called John turned towards her. "Tilly, how, what, where did you come from?" "Is it really you, John?" "Why of course it is honey, who else could be this ugly?" Tilly wrapped her arms around the man now known as John, as she sat upon the bench next to the barn, tears streaming down her face. "Oh John, it has been so long, and we didn't know, well, we didn't know if we would ever see you again."

By now, both Sarah and Kathy and the boys were still in the wagon, unaware of what was going on, as the wagon was on the other side of the barn. "Shouldn't we go see what is happening?" Sarah questioned, as she was a little uncomfortable with how long her mother had been gone. With that, they all climbed down from the wagon and began to walk around the barn, and suddenly, Sarah too, screamed, "Daddy, Daddy" and ran faster than a racehorse to where Tilly and John were. The soldier just stared in amazement as Sarah jumped into her father's lap, hugging him around the neck as tightly as she could. "Hold on girl," John spoke up. "I am a little sore and your hugging me just smarts a bit," he said with a broad grin on his face, hiding the pain he was experiencing as well as the joy of seeing his wife and little girl for the first time in two years.

Sally took the guard aside as best she could, and explained what was happening. He considered the situation, and said, "I am sorry, but he is still our prisoner. On the other hand, I hate to see a family all busted up, even if they are a Confederate one. I will have to report this to my commander, and he will have to decide what to do. With that, he motioned to another soldier nearby, explained to him about what was going on and instructed him to check with the captain, as he continued to stand guard, watching this very strange but certainly joyous reunion of father, mother, and daughter.

Shortly thereafter, Captain Burns, the commander of the troops guarding the Confederate prisoners, came around the corner with several other soldiers. He stopped a moment, looked at the group, and then spoke up: "Sir," speaking directly to John Woodbury, "I think I recognize you. You were in Pickett's last offensive, were you not?" John, concerned about admitting that he was, but being the honest man he had always been, said, "Yes sir, I was." Captain Burns continued, "That was a sorrowful mess, to be sure, but I remember seeing you near Emmitsburg Road." Fully aware that now everyone was listening, including Tilly and Sarah, and being a family man himself, he said: "What you did there was above and beyond the call of duty, regardless of which side you were on. I know that war is a horrible thing, and men do some pretty nasty things in war. But what you did in helping our injured troops, when your own life was at stake, is certainly worthy of mention to my superiors. With my recommendation, I am sure something can be worked out so you can return to your family."

Tilly and Sarah both took in what the Captain had said, then looked back at John who had tears in his eyes. "Oh, thank you," said Sarah, as she gave Captain Burns a hug. "That's alright young lady, I am just doing what is right and you should know how brave a man your poppa is." Sally reached over to Tilly and said, "I will leave you three here for a time. I am going to continue into town and will come back soon. You three visit, catch up a bit, and we can work out the details later. Sally drove off with her kids, and Captain Burns whispered to the soldier guarding the prisoners, "Give them some time; they are not going anywhere. I will be back in a bit." As he turned to leave, he looked back over his shoulder and saw the three in a family way, and wiped a tear from his own eye.

Section Thirty-Nine

Abigail Finds Another Rescue Effort

"Rachel, what do you say we go down to the military hospital?" Abigail suggested, as they were sitting around the kitchen table in the Handy house. "Now, why would we want to do that, Abigail?" Rachel replied. "Besides, we haven't found homes for these last few dogs I found while you were away!" "Well, I heard Mother and Father talking about how much help was needed with all the soldiers coming into town, you know, that ones that had been in battles. Washington has the best hospitals and all, and we could give them some help." "Abigail, we are not nurses, silly girl!" "I know, I know, but we can help with the supplies, cleaning up, helping the injured soldiers take walks. You know, little things that will let the nurses concentrate on the medical issues. Father said we got out of Gettysburg just in time; the three-day battle there was really horrible and there were a lot of casualties, on both sides. I just thought we could do our share. And besides, we can take a break from our animal friends for a while," said Abigail.

Abigail didn't tell Rachel how bored she had been since she had come back to Washington. Being away, even for the short time that they spent in Gettysburg, had opened her eyes a bit wider about what the world was all about, outside of her own house and street. There was so much going on in the country and she wanted to find out more. It also didn't hurt that she had met the Union soldier boy. She had never felt that way before; it gave her tingles just to think about him and his smile as she said goodbye. She often thought about him after that; what was he doing, and whether he was safe.

"Abigail, didn't you hear me?" shouted Rachel. "I have been trying to get through that thick skull of yours for over a minute. I don't know about the hospital; I will have to ask my parents. Besides, does this have anything to do with that soldier you met?" Abigail just blushed, looked away and replied," No, of course not. I was just thinking about how much we could help. It's been too hot to do much else in this town, so we might as well do something to help others. Besides, we have saved as many strays as we could by now," Abigail said firmly, a firmness that Rachel knew all too well. She knew that when Abigail had her mind made up, there wasn't much reason to argue with her.

"I will ask my parents later and let you know tomorrow," Rachel offered. "I am sure that they wouldn't mind, but they have to say yes first." With that, Rachel skipped out of the house and Abigail walked into the living room where Robert was cleaning and straightening the furniture. After the social that the Handys had the night before, the house needed tidying up, and Robert hated to let things go to the last minute.

He thought about what he had heard as he was serving the guests. Gettysburg was indeed a disaster for all the soldiers that either perished or were wounded. But, it did provide the supporters of the Union with some confidence about the progress of the war. Mr. Handy had talked to his guests about how he had talked to President Lincoln, and described the president's somber, yet encouraging words about his military leaders, and the victories at Gettysburg and also Vicksburg. As Robert heard these words, he could not help but think, once again, about his family, his real family. Not wanting to reveal his feelings, he quickly went back into the kitchen, to follow up on his chores, wondering to himself whether he still had a family.

"Robert, I am still waiting for an answer!" Abigail said as she put her hands on her hips and just stood there. "Why, what on earth do you mean, Missy?" Robert responded, in a questioning manner, yet in the back of his mind he knew what she meant. "Sit down here a minute, Abigail," and Robert motioned to the high-backed chair next to the table. "I suppose it is time that we talked." And with that, Robert related the adventures of his childhood, his life as a young slave, how he grew to be a man on that southern plantation and eventually, how he had to leave and finally how he had met her father.

"Oh Robert," Abigail said so sorrowfully, as she got up from her chair and gave him a hug. "I am sure that someday you will find out what happened to your family. I am sure that this war will not go on forever, and when it does end, and the Union wins, why, I'll bet slavery will be finally over too." Robert had to turn away and as he looked out the window, dabbing his eyes with the dish towel, he said, both to himself and to Abigail, "I am sure it will, Missy, I am sure it will.

Section Forty

Martin and Joshua Journey to Washington and Make Discoveries

The journey from Gettysburg to Washington, with its changing trains, smoke filled cars, stifling hot air, and less than smooth ride, was not easy for Martin. He thought of his friend Ollie often and was grateful that he himself only suffered an arm wound. It was enough, however, for Lieutenant Wilson to have him shipped to the hospital in Washington. He didn't know, and wouldn't find out for a while, that Joshua, despite being assigned to the cooking crew at Gettysburg, had also suffered a wound as the troops were forced to leave their camp and move. Joshua had been shot in the upper leg, was unable to walk and although the doctor in Gettysburg didn't think he would lose his leg, he thought that the best thing to do would be to ship him back to Washington where he would receive better medical care. Lieutenant Wilson had grown to like Joshua, and saw to it that he left as soon as possible. As luck would have it, he was on the same train with Martin, albeit in a different railroad car.

When the train arrived in Washington, and all the injured soldiers disembarked, Martin saw Joshua on a gurney and despite his own injury, hurried over to him. Their eyes made contact and Joshua said, "Martin, I can't believe you are alright. When you didn't come back to camp, I thought for sure you were gone. I heard about your friend Ollie, though. I am really sorry about his passing." At the mention of Ollie's name, Martin grew speechless. Joshua, noting his friend's reaction, then said, "But we are here, aren't we? We are going to be fine."

Later that day, they both were taken to the hospital, and along with hundreds of other wounded soldiers, with any number of different kinds of injuries, were placed in a ward. With the urging of Lieutenant Wilson, they were placed next to each other, and although Joshua was black, there were several black soldiers there as well, for the Union had opened up its ranks to black soldiers for some time. Still, he wasn't used to being with so many white people, as he remembered his time on the plantation. He began to miss his mother once again, and even old Mr. Washington. He thought about what would happen to him, once he was healed. Would he be sent back to the Andrews plantation? He just didn't know.

Abigail had gotten approval from her parents to visit the hospital, and along with Rachel, who also had gotten approval from her parents, they both were taken by Robert in the wagon to the hospital. Mrs. Handy had told Robert to make sure the girls got there safely, as the streets of Washington were just filled with all sorts of people and the crowds were suffocating. "Robert," Mrs.

Handy said to Robert as they were getting into the wagon, "Abigail and Rachel are young girls, and may not be ready to see all the horrible injuries that our brave soldiers received." Mr. Handy said that the less severely injured soldiers were placed in a separate section of the hospital; he just wasn't sure which one that would be. "Mrs. Handy, I will make sure that their young eyes are shielded from the worst cases. I have a friend who is an orderly at the hospital, and he can direct us to the proper place. I know the girls want to help out, which is right kindly of them, and they shouldn't have to spend their first day seeing the worst."

As they arrived at the hospital, Robert told the girls to wait in the wagon while he checked with his friend where to go. He walked in, and both girls looked at each other, and then began looking around the grass yards around the hospital. It was hot as usual for a summer day in Washington, and there were crowds of soldiers, nurses, volunteers and men with suits scattered around the grounds, drinking lemonade and cold water, talking to each other. It seemed like it was just another day, except for all the bandages that they could see.

As Robert came out from the front door of the hospital, he called out, "Girls, come on down and please tie up the horse for me. We can go into this wing on the left." The girls tied up the horse and walked up the stairs, following Robert into the hospital.

What they saw inside was not unlike what they saw outside, except they could now smell the smell of medicine, of rotting flesh, and the stench of War. They both had to hold their handkerchiefs against their noses to protect them from the smells. "Well girls, here we are," said the orderly as he accompanied Robert and the girls down the hallway of the first wing. "If you are going to volunteer to help out here, you might as well get used to what you see and smell. It doesn't get any better, although most of the boys here are not really badly injured. They need some cheering up, and I bet you two are just the ones to do that."

Abigail and Rachel held each other's hand, rather stiffly, as they walked from bed to bed, saying hello to the soldiers. They were of all ages, some young, almost as young as the girls, and some rather grizzled veterans. Robert and the orderly walked behind them, letting the girls be the first to see the soldiers in their beds.

As they neared the end of the wing, and before they got to the back door, Abigail thought she recognized a face. As she stepped forward, she cried out, "Martin, is that you?" Martin turned to face Abigail, remembering where he had seen her, and remembered the piece of paper he had stuffed into the pocket of his pants. "I sure do," responded Martin. "I would like to sit up and shake your hand, if I could," he said jokingly, showing Abigail his bandaged right arm. "Hey, I know what you can do for me, if of course you don't mind," Martin offered. Abigail spoke up: "Mr. Martin, or should I call you soldier, or Martin, or….". "Just call me Martin," he interrupted, and added, "Could you write a letter for me. I want to let my father know that I am fine. I understand that they will discharge me soon because of my injury and I want him to know that I will be coming home in a relatively short time."

Abigail nodded and sat down next to the bed, and with a pen and paper provided by the orderly, she began to write. She then stopped a moment and said to Martin, "if you would like, I can talk to my father. Maybe you could stay in Washington a while and the Army can find another position for you. My father knows quite a few people in this town, and who knows, you might be able to stay." Martin thought to himself a bit about the possibility of staying in Washington, not going home right away, a thought that seemed quite nice, as Abigail returned to her paper and pen.

Now, as she did so, and the orderly stepped out of the way, Robert noticed that there was a black soldier next to Martin. He stepped over next to him and took a seat on the chair next to the bed, and asked him his name. "Joshua, sir." And what is yours? Robert thought it unusual that this boy would be so responsive, but he said, "Robert is my name." "Where are you from, Joshua?" "Oh, I am from a long way from here Mr. Robert. From South Carolina."

"My, my, you are a long way from home, Joshua. And by the way, you can call me Robert." "I assume you are a free man, Joshua, since you are here in the Union uniform?" "No, sir, I mean yes sir," Joshua stammered, as he wasn't sure what he was! Robert wasn't sure why, or what was motivating him, but he was beginning to take an interest in this young man, and as long as Abigail was busy writing the letter for Martin, he continued to talk to Joshua. "Now, tell me how you got to be in the Union army, Joshua. I don't mean to be nosy, but its mighty unusual for a black boy to be up here like this."

Joshua began telling Robert his story, and as he did so, Robert stiffened and began to shake inside. Joshua could sense that something was wrong, and asked Robert what was bothering him. Robert could barely speak, and his mouth was getting dry, but he asked Joshua what his mother's name was. "Why it was

Mattie, sir," Joshua responded. Robert's eyes began to tear, and his whole body began to shake. As he pulled out his handkerchief, he asked another question: "Joshua, what was the name of your plantation? "Joshua responded, "Why, it was the Andrews plantation, sir."

Robert jumped up and with a rush of energy, called out, "Hallelujah, hallelujah." His sudden burst of energy caused everyone around to stop and look. Abigail stopped writing, and the orderly came up to Robert and asked him if he was alright. He had never seen Robert so boisterous before as he was normally very restrained in his relations. "Alright?" "No, I am not alright," Robert exclaimed. "I am overcome with emotion and I can barely restrain myself."

As he said this, he asked Joshua one more question. "Now Joshua, did your momma tell you anything about your father, anything at all?" "Well, I told you he had to leave the plantation real, quick like. She did say though that he was a big, strong man and once was in a scuffle with the overseer and got cut. He had a big scar on the side of...."

As Joshua spoke, Robert turned to the side, and Joshua saw that Robert had a big scar on the side of his face, just where his mother had said it was. By now, tears were streaming down Robert's face and his body was moving side to side. The orderly whispered into Robert's ear, "Is this...?" Robert whispered back, "It has to be. My woman was named Mattie and we lived on the Andrews plantation in South Carolina before I was sold off."

Robert turned once again to Joshua, who by now was sitting up in his bed, turning first to Martin, then to Robert, then to Martin again, then to Robert again. "I don't understand, sir, I mean Robert?" "Joshua," Robert, gathering himself and speaking in a slow, deliberate manner: "You are my son, Joshua, my own flesh and blood." And with that, Robert reached down and gave Joshua the biggest hug he could possibly give. He had finally reached the end of his journey, to find his family, and although Mattie was now gone, something he would or could never forget, he finally had his son. He slowly pushed himself away from Joshua, and they both looked into each other's eyes with a knowing, with an understanding, that each of them was now "home."

Made in the USA
Middletown, DE
12 September 2021